YOU'VE GOT SPELLS

CHRISTINE ZANE THOMAS

Copyright © 2021 by Christine Zane Thomas

All rights reserved.

No part of this book may be reproduced in any form or by any electronic or mechanical means, including information storage and retrieval systems, without written permission from the author, except for the use of brief quotations in a book review.

Cover designed by William Tyler Davis using Deposit Photos stock.

❦ Created with Vellum

For Summer. You crazy.

1

IN WITCH WE MAKE COFFEE

"**M**agic sucks!" I put it so eloquently—and loud enough for the whole shop to hear.

But no one within earshot batted an eye. They knew. They understood. Magic was annoying and finicky. Sometimes its rules were hard and fast—like the rule requiring a great need to use it. Other times, it flowed straight from my fingertips without me giving it much thought.

It wasn't easy. Not that I would've expected it to be. Nor had I expected for magic to be real.

That was, until a cat spoke to me. My grandmother's cat to be precise. My grandmother's familiar, Stevie, to be more precise.

At the time, Gran had been trying to tell me the truth—that, like my mother and her and her mother and her mother's mother, I'm a witch. I come from a long line of witches. And, like them, magic began to flow from my fingertips when I reached the age of forty.

A whole bunch of other, equally crazy things happened after that—including several of my matrilineal ancestresses' memories flashing before my eyes. At the time, I was trapped inside my own mind by what else? Magic.

Not exactly an experience I wanted to relive. In fact, a lot of things had happened over the past few months that I'd love to block out. They all had to do with magic.

"Magic doesn't suck." Trish rolled her eyes—it's kind of her thing.

Those eyes were outlined in black eyeliner with wings, matching her wardrobe—all black, from her shirt down to her boots. The only pop of color, save her green eyes, was a streak of violet in her otherwise, you guessed it, black as night hair.

"Easy for you to say," I shot back. "You know what your gift is. And every spell you try turns up rainbows and unicorns."

Trish was the closest thing I had to a best friend in this town. She was also the owner of Bewitched Books, where I worked.

I ground my teeth in frustration. For such a crazy expensive piece of machinery, this thing was a struggle to make work.

"Work, damn you."

While not exactly a magic spell, it proved effective. The new espresso machine—the one we'd bid on and won at the last police auction—began to gurgle and hiss.

"No such thing as unicorns, I'm afraid." Trish smirked. Sometimes she made it really difficult to be her friend.

It was my turn to roll my eyes, which had nowhere near as much makeup. Also, they're a soft blue, not green.

At the register, Trish took a sip from a cup of tea. She'd brewed it in protest, a jab at my coffeemaking skills.

"Okay, Miss English Breakfast," I said. "If you think you can do so much better, why don't you give it a try?"

She shook her head. "No. This was your idea. No reason I should get dragged into it."

I started frothing milk, yelling over the loud hiss. "It's your store. I thought this might drum up some business."

"And I appreciate that. I really do. But my cup is kind of full right now."

I hate puns when puns are directed at me.

Trish flipped the violet streak out of her face. Her way of saying, "See how clever I am." Another witch, and a soon-to-be witch, but not too soon, laughed. They waited while I tried to figure out the machine.

It was the first monthly meeting of the witches since the neighboring coffee shop, Brew at the Burrow, had closed—and since one of our cohorts, Kalene Moone, left town. She and Ivan Rush were fulfilling their duties with the Faction, a not-so-nefarious underground organization of witches. The current membership was two and a half, counting me as the half.

Lauren Whittaker and her daughter, Merritt, chatted quietly. They sat in the new armchairs beside the front window—bought online, not at the police auction. To make this happen, we'd moved several bookshelves to the other side of the store and brought the aisles closer together by a few inches.

I called it cozy. Trish said it brought on her claustrophobia when she perused the shelves. She thought it would put off customers. I pointed out that we didn't have many customers. At least not yet.

The new seating, along with the espresso machine and fridge, were all part of my plan to revamp and rebrand Bewitched Books. I wanted customers. And deep down, I knew Trish did too.

Her relationship with her boss at the grocery store,

Jade Gerwig, had hit a tipping point with the craziness that happened at After Dark Con. Not only had the gathering of paranormal enthusiasts drawn many visitors to our town, but a presentation had also put us in real danger.

Jade, one of the organizers of the event and cohost of the *Creel Creek After Dark* podcast, had always maintained a rocky but professional relationship with Trish. It was when Jade and her crony, Summer Shields, offered us up to a hypnotist who locked us into our minds that she'd done something unforgivable.

Now Trish needed an exit strategy from her regular job as the assistant manager at the grocery. I was hoping this could be it. That was, if I could get the stupid espresso machine to work.

To the best of my abilities, I finished the milk and poured Lauren and Merritt's drinks. A mocha and a caramel macchiato. Both with generous helpings of syrup.

Like the drinks, the two women had their similarities but were altogether different. Over forty but with the appearance of a teenager, Lauren was dark-haired and fair-skinned with freckles across the bridge of her nose and cheeks. Her large blue eyes were expressive and kind. Merritt also had blue eyes. She was taller than her mother. Tan and rail thin.

Lauren took a hesitant sip from the cup I'd given her. Her already big blue eyes went wider. "It's a good first attempt."

It was my twentieth attempt. They just hadn't been there for the others.

"Yeah," Merritt muttered into her drink. "It's a good thing the closest Starbucks is over an hour away."

"Why do you say it like that?" Lauren asked her.

"Because no one here will know the difference between..." She winced.

"Go on," I said. "I can take it."

"Can you though?" Trish asked.

I glowered at her then brightened, focusing again on Merritt. "Between what?"

"Between good coffee and, uh, not so good." She shielded her face from view with the cup.

"Told you you couldn't take it."

Magic flew from my fingertips, jolting Trish as if I'd dragged my feet across a shag carpet for five minutes then tapped her with my pointer finger.

Trish tried to respond in kind, but her magic disagreed with the use. "Curses, how is that fair?"

"Told you, magic sucks."

"Hey, uh, just leave me out of it. Okay?" Merritt rocked her chair, throwing her legs and arms up in an attempt to block any unseen magical force.

I wasn't planning to shoot anything her way. But she was lucky I only used my magic for good—or mostly good. A girl in her twenties, Merritt had over a decade before she came into her powers.

I laughed, shaking my head. "I'll wait till you can defend yourself. And it's not the coffee's fault. It's mine. I just don't understand how this machine works. It's like it's too fancy."

"Plus, you're not that good at multitasking." Trish was still trying to jinx me.

I sent another bolt her way.

"Ouch! That one really stung!"

"Thanks for the boost of confidence."

"It's the truth." She rubbed her arms gingerly. Her hair was wild with static. "I thought we said honesty is the best policy."

"You're too honest. All three of you. Let's revise the policy until after I figure out this machine."

"Oh, come on. It can't be that hard."

Trish scooted into the enclosed space behind the espresso machine with me.

I took my terribly made latte from earlier and went behind the register to watch from afar—and also to monitor for hexes. I'd just gotten settled when the door swung open and the chime went off.

All four of us stared. While the sign read open, there was hardly ever a visitor this early in the morning. And I wasn't advertising the new coffee and tea menu yet.

Nevertheless, a woman with a cheerful smile stopped about a foot inside the store. She wore jeans and a cardigan with leather Oxford shoes so cute I wanted to ask her where she'd bought them.

If she was uneasy at the four of us staring at her, she didn't show it. She took in her surroundings, pausing to smile at each of the two witches lounging in the front of the store. She gave a final lingering smile to me but failed to notice Trish, whose short stature made her near-impossible to find behind the coffee counter and espresso machine.

"Hello, ladies," she said. "Beautiful day, isn't it?"

Lauren and Merritt smiled in agreement.

I raised an eyebrow. "Can I help you?"

"I hope so," she said. "The last time I passed through town, there was a coffee shop down at the end of the strip. It's boarded up now. I was wondering if y'all knew anything about that—or perhaps where I could get a latte this morning." She gave the giant espresso machine a longing look. "And now I see you might be able to offer me one yourselves..."

"Looks can be deceiving," Merritt joked.

Lauren waggled a finger and Merritt rocketed upward, as if a jolt of electricity had zipped up her spine. One probably had.

"I could try," Trish said without much conviction.

"Is that you, Great and Powerful Oz?" The woman straightened, bobbing on tiptoe to see around the machine.

"Listen, funny girl," Trish poked her head out, her green eyes blazing, "we just got this thing. I haven't even touched it yet. But I'm willing to give it a go if you're up for it. And, because I'm being nice, I'll give it to you half price. What would you like?"

"Wait." The woman's forehead creased. "What do you mean by you haven't touched it yet?"

"I made the other drinks," I chimed in.

"Then maybe you should—"

"No!" Lauren and Merritt were quick to say. Too quick. I swirled my finger and they both sat up straighter.

"Let Trish try," Lauren mumbled through the shock. "Trust me."

"That bad, eh?" She screwed up her face.

"I'm still learning," I protested.

"Nothing a few YouTube videos can't resolve." The woman sauntered—actually sauntered to the coffee counter. She put her elbows on the counter and leaned toward Trish. "Do you mind if I help? I'll pay. But maybe I could show you two how it's done."

I thought Trish might clock her. "What makes you so sure you can?"

"I was a barista in college." She dimpled. "I think I've still got the knowhow buried somewhere in here." She tapped the tight curls on her head.

"And what do you do these days?" Trish asked her. "Miss...Misses..."

"Castel. Jami Castel." She flashed her pearly whites again, as genuinely as before or even more so. "Sorry, that's the best Bond impression I've got. And I'm not a spy. I'm a freelancer, mostly. I'm writing a piece on the Late Harvest Festival for *Virginia Vines Magazine*. Have you heard of it?"

Trish stepped back, making room for her in the small space between the counter and the wall. "I've heard of the Late Harvest Festival."

Jami shrugged like it was the news she'd expected. "It's a new magazine. Digital only... for now."

"Neat," Lauren said. She was also being genuine.

Jami went to work. She took the portafilter and filled it with ground espresso. She leveled the grounds and tamped them firmly, but not too firmly. "The trick is not to pack it too loose or too tight. You'll have to gauge it for yourselves, though."

Trish nodded. "So, why is *Virginia Vines* interested in Creel Creek's harvest festival?"

"Honestly?" For the first time, Jami looked like she had trepidations, as if she were about to divulge a big secret. "I'm sort of the owner of *Virginia Vines*. When I heard that Armand Vineyards was hosting the event, it just made sense to drive over."

Jami plugged the portafilter into the machine. "They make good wine. And they aren't usually open to the public."

"We're aware," I said.

We were all too aware. My friend, Cyrus, owned the vineyard, among other things. I hadn't spoken to him in a while, but Dave had been prepping for the Late Harvest Festival for weeks. I'd promised his girls I would take them while their dad worked.

"Yeah. I talked the owner into an interview today," Jami

went on. "Of course I'll be back for the main event tomorrow. It's all a bit strange. Most small towns have their harvest festivals sometime in October, when the weather is getting good. You know, making the switch to chilly mornings and cool nights with comfortable midday temperatures, not too sweltering. November is so iffy up here. We'll be lucky if that cold front doesn't blow through."

She was right. October was a better month. But most towns aren't Creel Creek, where Main Street is dilapidated and the only two shops either sell tobacco or are filled with spell books and grimoires. Creel Creek, Virginia is full of paranormal beings—witches like me and the others, werewolves like Dave and his sister Imogene, along with shifters of every variety.

It made sense for us to do things differently. Halloween is a scary time in the paranormal community. It's the day of the year that the spell cast on the town is broken. Creel Creek's regular citizens can see the *others* for what they truly are on the inside.

"I love Armand Wine," Merritt spoke up. She was barely old enough to drink it. She probably compared it against Two Buck Chuck and those fruity gas station wines most college-age girls drink.

Not that I claimed to be a sommelier. Far from it. *Pass the Arbor Mist.*

"It's the oldest winery in the region," Jami said.

"I didn't know that."

Merritt didn't. I knew. Cyrus had owned it since moving to the United States ages ago. Literal ages—being undead and all.

The espresso machine gurgled to life, and Jami pointed to the coffee trickling into her espresso shot glass. "You want this to layer into three shades. The darkest on the bottom. Lightest on top. Now, let's try the milk."

She showed us how to froth the milk without scalding it, then she made an impressive leaf with the pour. "That, my dears, will take some practice." She took a sip, satisfied. "What do I owe you?"

Trish shook her head, a look of almost admiration on her face. "It's free. It's us who owe you. Thanks for the lesson."

"Oh. That's kind of you. One final tip. You should get your own beans. The place over there roasted theirs. It really adds that extra touch."

"We'll take it into consideration." Trish's face soured. Jami had taken her advice that one step too far. We were a bookshop, after all—and one that dealt mostly in magic. Not a coffee shop.

Trish waited for her to leave and said, "Well, wasn't she a peach?"

"She seemed nice enough to me," Merritt said.

"She did show us how to use the espresso machine." I scooted in beside her, wanting to use my newfound knowledge.

"She was showing off," Trish complained. "And there was something else odd about her. Did you feel it?"

"Feel what?" Merritt asked.

I shrugged.

"Well," Trish glanced around the room, ensuring we had our listening ears on, "I told you about my new power…"

"The sensitivity thing?" Lauren asked.

"That's it." Trish nodded. "I think maybe I could feel something with her."

Each month, we held a circle. A more formal gathering under the crescent moon at midnight—the witching hour.

At our last circle, each of us had been given a gift from the mother herself, Mother Gaia.

Now, every witch can sense magic, sometimes when we touch each other, but mostly we can feel magic when it's used, like a sort of hum in the air. Trish's gift gave her enhanced magical awareness. To her, magic had frequency, and every practitioner emitted their own music.

When she'd figured it out, she said mine was like an out of tune heavy metal band. Not exactly a compliment, especially when compared to Gran's, which she said was like an orchestra warming up.

I still didn't know what gift I'd been given, if anything. Neither did Lauren.

"It was definitely something," Trish said. "Some sort of magic."

"Are you saying she's a witch?" I asked.

"No. Not exactly. I think maybe she's just sensitive."

"Sensitive like how?"

"Well, not everyone is like us, right? You remember that guy at After Dark Con? What was his name?"

"Josh?" I offered.

"Right. Josh. Part Fae or fairy or whatever. But he never knew it because that story got buried in the past somehow. His mother's mother's mother didn't tell her daughter or whatever. The same goes with magic. It can die out."

"Except with Jami Castel… it's not dead?"

"Right. Well, sort of. It's not there though. She doesn't have the magic. But if she could find it somehow, she could use it."

"I don't understand."

"I'm not explaining it right," Trish said. "Sorry. This stuff is new to me too."

"Have you run across many other people like that?" Lauren asked her.

"It's Creel Creek," Trish scoffed. "Of course I have. I thought I was going mad at first. It's how I figured out my gift. You wouldn't believe how many people I cross paths with at the grocery, and so many are harboring secrets."

"Secrets they know nothing about..." I tamped espresso in the portafilter just as Jami Castel had.

"That's kind of sad." Merritt frowned.

It was. She had been close to a similar fate. Had she not met us and reconnected with Lauren, Merritt might never have understood her magic when she turned forty. Instead, she was years ahead of the curve. Years ahead of me, anyway.

"It is sad," Trish agreed. "But I think it's part of how everyone ends up here in Creel Creek. They're drawn here by something."

"By magic." I finished making a new drink, a simple latte this time. No latte art. It was just a blob of foam on the top of the drink.

"I like magic," Lauren said thoughtfully.

"I like it too," I agreed begrudgingly. "Except when it sucks and is overly complicated. And when it does things I'll never understand."

Trish rolled her eyes and raised her tea. "To magic."

"To magic." We clinked, without actually *clinking,* our paper cups. My latte didn't taste half bad either.

2

CREEL CREEK AFTER DARK
EPISODE 76

It's getting late.
Very late.
The creeping dread of tomorrow haunts your dreams.
It's dark out. Are you afraid?
Welcome to Creel Creek After Dark.

Ivana: Happy birthday to you, you live in a zoo. You might be turning forty, but you're hot like twenty-two.

Athena: You think of that yourself?

Ivana: Oh, no, I had help.

Athena: From?

Ivana: A ghostwriter, actually. They prefer to remain anonymous.

Athena: Interesting... because today, we welcome a ghostwriter to the show. Could the two be one and the same? Or is that where you got the idea to hire a ghost?

Ivana: Clever guesses. But no. They are not one and the same. Fine, I'll tell you—I thought that jingle up myself. You're so surprised, aren't you?

Athena: Not in the slightest, Ivana! Welcome, everyone,

to *Creel Creek After Dark*! I'm your now over-the-hill hostess, Athena Hunter.

Ivana: And I'm her been over-the-hill-and-tumbled-down-it cohost, Ivana Steak. This is episode seventy-six for those keeping track.

Athena: I don't feel any different, turning forty.

Ivana: You won't. Besides, forty is the new thirty.

Athena: Everyone said the same thing when I turned thirty. It was the new twenty. So, does that mean forty is the new twenty? Or is twenty back in its rightful place? I'm not sure how that works. I'm not that good at math.

Ivana: Nor am I. But if I had to guess, I'd say you're tracking no higher than twenty-nine on the "how old do you look" chart.

Athena: Funny story! I took a quiz the other day that was supposed to guess my age.

Ivana: And?

Athena: Fifty. What can I say? I'm an old soul.

Ivana: We both are. In fact, it's something I find endearing about you—the way you cozy up at night with a book and tea. Isn't that how you discovered our next guest?

Athena: Nice segue. And yes, that is how I spend most nights. Although it's getting to be hot cocoa weather. Not tea. I checked these particular books out from the local library, and the librarian, Rowena—a former guest on our show—mentioned she knew the author. And guess what? They're local. I cried foul.

Ivana: Because the name on the cover is different?

Athena: That's the reason. The "author" is a well-known figure in the paranormal community.

Ivana: But he doesn't write his own books.

Athena: Apparently not. Let's get into the interview and shed some light on this after a break for our sponsor...

Man's Voice: *The Creel Creek Annual Late Harvest Festival is right around the corner. Come out, everyone, for fun, games, and prizes. There will be rides, food, and the third largest corn maze in the state. See you this Saturday outside Armand Vineyards.*

Ivana: Welcome, listeners, back to the show. And welcome to the show.

Ghost: Thank you! Glad to be here.

Athena: From now on, we'll be referring to you as ghost. Is that all right?

Ghost: I've been called worse.

Athena: Haven't we all? What's your favorite insult?

Ivana: Athena! Let's not go there.

Athena: Right. Sorry... I've been going through a rough patch recently. Let's start off with a little about you. You're from around here?

Ghost: I am. I grew up in Creel Creek, got my degree and a master's degree in history from University of Virginia. I returned here to teach at the high school.

Ivana: How did you get into ghostwriting?

Ghost: It's a long and boring story. Here are the highlights: I, like almost everyone my age, got interested in genealogy at some point. This was before that awful website came along. I did a great deal of research. I found some of my ancestors had quite colorful pasts, and I attempted to write about them. I sent my story to an agent, who wasn't interested in my family's past, but he knew someone looking for a "writing partner," as he called it.

Athena: Is that how you see it? A partnership?

Ghost: Heavens, no. I do the research. I write the words. I get paid.

Ivana: And *he* gets all the glory?

Ghost: If you want to call it that, yes. His name is on the cover.

Athena: Did your original story ever get published?

Ghost: No, it did not.

Ivana: Can you tell us more about the books?

Ghost: Unfortunately, no. I don't want to make it too easy for your listeners to put two and two together. I can't tell you what books I've written or not written. It's part of my contract, a nondisclosure agreement.

Athena: But it's fair to say that a few have been about supernatural phenomena?

Ghost: Correct. There are hints of the supernatural in my work.

Athena: And at least one book was set here in town?

Ghost: As I said, I grew up here. I have a soft spot for Creel Creek and Virginia in general. But not everything I write is set here.

Ivana: Some are...

Ghost: Yes. The one, like you say. But again, we can't say the title publicly. At least not without a lawsuit and a lawsuit from my publisher.

Ivana: We don't want that.

Athena: Without the titles, or specifics, I'd like to speak on a few of your books. I've read them all, I think, and they're so insightful. You're like us, you're after the truth.

Ghost: I make a point to offer only facts in my work. I leave the speculation to the readers. No offense.

Athena: None taken. We find it's best if we encourage our listeners along. Sometimes we have to do the math for them, if you will.

Ghost: Oh, I understand completely. My readers and your listeners are a lot alike. They understand that two plus two is four. But they may not remember much algebra.

When two plus X is equal to four, X is equal to two. But when we throw in another value, Y, in our equation, things get complicated.

Ivana: Sometimes, we postulate what Y might be and leave them to calculate X.

Athena: My head's spinning from so much math talk. It's like eighth grade all over again. Let's remind our listeners about the show sponsor.

Ivana: Today's sponsor is, if you'll believe it, the town of Creel Creek. This year's annual Late Harvest Festival is right around the corner. Get your tickets online and save five dollars. All proceeds go to the courthouse restoration project.

Ivana: We'll be there.

Athena: That's right! I wouldn't miss it. Nobody stands between me and a funnel cake or three.

Ivana: Oh my gosh! How do you eat those things?

Athena: It's fried and covered in sugar. That's like the epitome of easy to eat cuisine.

Ivana: Sounds like the epitome of a stomachache.

Athena: I guess we'll just have to agree to disagree. Ghost, what do you think about funnel cake?

Ghost: I think I've made a poor judgment call agreeing to this interview. If you'll excuse me...

3

IN WITCH A GRAVE IS ROBBED

The problem with daylight savings isn't the additional hours in summer when the sunsets occur so late. No, the problem is how it cashes out those savings in the fall.

It was like midnight stepping outside at the end of my shift, except it was just past six o'clock. The sky was pitch black with no stars. A single light pole in the gravel lot behind the store illuminated the dumpster with pale orange light.

Perched on the lamp in statuesque fashion was my usual visitor. I threw the day's waste in the open flap, and the owl let out a low hoot in reply. She ruffled her feathers and followed me toward my car, swooping silently to the roof rails atop Prongs, my Subaru Outback.

"Hello, friend."

The owl made a tutting sound.

For a week or two, I called the owl Mom. She wasn't liking the downgrade.

But there was nothing doing. I'd tried about every spell I could think of, and some that I couldn't, to change her back, believing that it was actually my mother trapped in the body and mind of an owl.

Either I was wrong or my magic wasn't strong enough to reverse the spell... or a combination of both.

There was definitely something strange about this owl. Twice, it had aided me in a time of need. It was an ever-present shadow since I'd moved to Creel Creek, following me everywhere I went. I had it on good authority that its thoughts weren't like other owls'. They were more human.

In my first month in Creel Creek, I'd seen humans that were transformed into animals. I'd even changed one back accidentally.

That spell hadn't worked on this owl. Nothing had.

And everyone—Gran, Trish, Lauren, and Dave—thought I was crazy to suspect the owl of being my mother. An ally, sure. But nothing more. Even my own familiar, Brad, who shared a special bond with me, wasn't convinced.

My own belief had waned. Sort of. Hence the demotion to friend. Still, a small part of me, something deep in the recesses of my mind, continued to believe. I just no longer voiced that opinion.

Maybe it was that I hated to admit I was no closer to solving the mystery of my mother's disappearance. Maybe I just hated being wrong. That was definitely true. No one likes being wrong. But that wasn't really it. I just refused to give up hope.

"Still talking to that thing?" Brad clambered into the car.

"I talk to all sorts of nuisance animals," I said. "Where've you been all day? I was about to leave you."

"Special mission in the shadow realm. You'll thank me later."

"Good night," I told the owl.

She flew silently over the store, toward the courthouse,

in the direction of Gran's house. I cranked the car and Brad climbed into the backseat. We followed the owl.

"What do you mean by special mission?" I asked.

"You remember the demon who held me captive—the one you're going to set free in a few months?"

"For a day," I said. "I'm setting him free for a day."

"That's assuming he sticks to the bargain and doesn't manage an escape. And that you can bind him after said twenty-four hours. That's a lot of assuming."

"I get it. But we have over six months to figure that out."

"You realize I've gotten to know you, right? Six months to figure it out—you'll remember the day of—if we're lucky. Hence why I've started to work it out for you."

"You have?"

"Preliminary work. It's a shame the shadow realm is off limits to you lot. We could cover a lot more ground, so to speak."

"What kind of ground do we need to cover?"

"All of it," Brad said.

"All of it, all of it?" The shadow realm is more than just a realm. It's the shadow of our world with portals—doors that open into infinite other worlds.

"Just the in-between world, the shadow realm itself," Brad said. "The trick will be for one of us—Twinkie or me, Stevie, if we can convince him—to keep tabs on him from there. When time's up, we'll lure him into a circle either there or here."

"Easier said than done." I sighed. I didn't want to think about this, not yet. Brad was right. I'd put it off until the day of if I could. "Can I ask you something?"

"There's an obvious answer to that," he said. "I'm your familiar. It's basically my job to answer your questions."

"I know. I just wasn't sure how to frame it."

"Go on."

"Have you looked at the owl from the shadow realm?"

"I have." His head appeared above the console between the seats. "You aren't going to like my answer."

"Never mind. I won't ask it."

He disappeared into the darkness of the backseat.

The highway was dark, trees lining most of it, with a random house tucked in every half mile or so. The light of Gran's subdivision, with its many houses and streetlamps, glowed in the distance.

But oddly, they weren't the only lights I saw. Inside the cemetery, just ahead of the turn, lights flashed blue. A sheriff's department SUV was parked next to one of the more prominent monuments amongst rows of smaller headstones.

"That's weird." I slammed on the brakes and swerved onto the side of the road in that direction. Prongs had no trouble navigating the bit of grass and rock that I'd carelessly mowed over. Brad wasn't as lucky. He went flying from the driver's side of the backseat to the passenger side.

"A warning would've been nice!"

"I keep telling you we should get you a harness."

"And I keep telling you I'm an immortal being sent to Earth to aid your witchy endeavors, not some cute pet."

"I never accused you of being cute." I smiled.

Easing past headstones on the hardened dirt drive, I stopped the car behind Dave's SUV. The overhead light popped on as I opened the door. Brad scooted up on his haunches in the seat, peering outside.

"Wait in the car," I told him.

"But I—"

"Wait in the car."

. . .

I was afraid my boyfriend, Dave Marsters, might think this was me being nosy. For all I knew, he'd pulled somebody over and they'd driven halfway down the cemetery road to get away from the highway. Why anyone would do such a thing, I couldn't fathom. But people do weird things when pulled over by the police. Every day, Dave came home with a story or two.

Tall and lean, with dark hair and eyes and a perpetual five o'clock shadow, Dave was everything I could want in a man. He was thoughtful and kind. Cute, when he wanted to be, and sexy when he didn't need to be. Dave knew when to say the right things and when not to say anything at all. And although he'd seen tragedy in his life and his work, his gorgeous smile came easily to his lips and stayed there often.

I could tell almost immediately this wasn't someone pulled over for speeding. There was no hint of that smile on Dave's lips, not even when he acknowledged me headed his way. He scuffed his work boots on the ground, kicking up loose dirt around what looked to be an empty grave.

The spotlight attached beside the mirror on the SUV's driver's side beamed away from the car. I came around to the other side and got a look at the scene.

On the other side of the grave, a man leaned on a beat-up shovel.

He was tall and lanky with a shaggy gray beard that met with hair of roughly the same length. The hair wrapped from his ears around his head but had receded so that only a few wisps remained on the top.

The man pointed in my direction, and Dave turned, shielding his eyes with a hand. He squinted through the spotlight's beam. "I was wondering if you'd show up."

"I just got off work. What's going on?" I folded my arms

against the chill and moved closer, but not too close, to the large pit.

"Constance, this is Griffin Barber—the cemetery's groundskeeper."

"That's right." Griffin Barber spat tobacco juice on the ground.

"Griffin, this is my girlfriend, Constance Campbell. She lives in the subdivision over there."

"Aye, I've seen her poking around here."

"I do not poke around here," I argued, taken aback not only by Griffin Barber's words but also his attitude. "I run along the fence."

"Same difference," he muttered.

"Griffin," Dave stifled a laugh, "I can assure you it wasn't Constance who did this."

"Oh, I know it wasn't." His voice maintained an edge. "It was those teenagers who did the spray painting at Halloween. They've gone and upped their game from pure vandalism to something more sinister."

I wasn't sure what had happened here, but the sight of an open grave was never a good one. "What'd they do?" I asked.

"Hold on." Dave used the same tone he reserved for all police business—skeptical but with authority. "We can't be sure it was them."

"What happened?" I asked again.

"This grave was robbed."

The spotlight illuminated the first few inches inside the grave. When I looked into it, there was nothing discernible but the dark, uneven walls of dirt and rock and a bottom that looked mostly the same.

Dave clicked on his flashlight and pointed it. What I'd failed to make out was the gleaming metal of an open casket, most of which was covered in dirt, much of which had found its way inside the cushioned interior.

What was noticeably missing was a human body.

"Oh," I gasped. "That's not good."

"Not good at all." Griffin reached down with his shovel, scraping the lid of the casket with a sound of metal on metal. It took him a moment to find the leverage he'd been searching for, and with a practiced motion, he pushed the lid closed. "I expect you'll find who did this?"

Griffin had leveled his gaze at Dave.

"I'll do my best. In the meantime, let me notify the family."

"No arguments there. I'm not even sure his family lives around here anymore. I wouldn't. I'd have gotten as far away from this place as I could."

Dave didn't offer a reply.

"Who is that?" I asked. "Anyone we know?"

Dave eyed me and shook his head, silently telling me it wasn't a subject he wanted to get into with Griffin Barber around. But I could read the headstone: Steven Robillard. July 14th, 1955 to November 22nd, 2010. And since I'd only been in Creel Creek a matter of months, there was no way I knew him.

"Anything else before I dig this thing up?" Griffin asked Dave, who again shook his head.

I went rigid. "You're going to dig it up? Why?"

"In hopes the owner is returned. After all, they were returned the last time this happened."

"Wait... this has happened in the past?"

"Several years ago." Griffin yanked up the shovel. "Not here, though. Taken from that graveyard up in there. It wasn't pretty. Took eight of them, if I recall. Found 'em in a mass grave out in these woods. Sheriff, you remember?"

Dave nodded. "I was pretty green back then."

"You sure were. But it was you who found 'em, wasn't it?"

"You've got a good memory. I got lucky."

"Maybe you'll get lucky again." He jabbed the shovel in the ground beside him. "And let's hope this will be the only dead body you find for a while. Lord knows we've seen enough recently."

Dave grunted in reply.

I had to agree. The town had a seen a number of deaths in the short time I'd lived there. From Mr. Caulfield, the vampire grocery store manager, to the most recent slaying of three elders at the League of Artemis, a fraternal order of shifters. And that wasn't counting the death of their slayer... by my hand.

"I'll leave you to it," Dave told Griffin. He put a hand at the small of my back and walked with me to the car.

"I guess dinner's off?" I asked.

"Are you kidding? I'm not fooling around with this tonight."

I smiled and pecked him on the lips. "Meet at your house in fifteen?"

He smiled back. "I can get there in five with my lights on."

"You wouldn't." I laughed.

"No. You're right. I wouldn't."

He opened the door for me.

"What *did* happen last time?" I asked in a whisper.

"Let's just say I didn't get lucky finding those bodies. My nose—my heightened sense of smell—led the way."

"And?"

He shrugged. "And that's about all there is to tell. I found the missing bodies. But we never found who was responsible. Or why."

4

IN WITCH I SLEEP LIKE THE DEAD

"I'm just popping in to drop off a few things."

I passed Gran in the kitchen on my way to the laundry room off the garage. I threw my clothes from the dryer into the hamper and hung up my shirts. It only took a few minutes—the beauty of laundry for one.

I dropped the hamper in my room upstairs and returned to the kitchen, where I checked the fridge. Not that I needed anything. It was habit—a bad habit. What else is there to do in a kitchen aside from forage for food?

It didn't help that Gran never told me when she was out of things, expecting me to *automagically* sense when she needed half-and-half or butter. I made a mental note—she needed everything.

"I thought you were just popping in." Stevie's booming voice filled the nook in the kitchen. The large black cat, Gran's familiar, sprang up on the chair beside hers. "Does this mean you're staying for dinner?"

"No." I closed the fridge. "To be honest, there's not much in there for dinner."

"If you must know," Gran muttered, "I'm having something delivered."

"What? Pizza?"

"Something." She shrugged. "What's it matter to you? You won't be here. We *know* the routine, don't we fellas? Popping in to pop out again. We hardly see you anymore."

"I don't have to go, if you don't want me to..."

"No, no. I'm not complaining. You go." She never looked my direction. She sat at the kitchen table, pretending to work on a puzzle. "In fact, I like it better with you gone."

"You know, it wasn't so long ago, you were trying to kick me out. Do I sense a change of heart?"

"Oh, no. It's fine by me. Go on, live your life. I got along well enough for eighty-eight years without you. I can do a few more."

I scowled. It was hard to tell when she was lying to get a rise out of me—or telling the truth to get a rise out of me.

Or both.

Gran hunched over her puzzle, a Paris street café with the Eiffel Tower in the background, five hundred pieces. The edges were done, and pieces were scattered around a hefty stack of mail, old coffee cups, and spent dishes.

"We talk about you when you're gone," Stevie said.

"You do not."

"We do," Brad corroborated. He found his usual spot, on the floor beside the kibble.

Gran shrugged again, holding a puzzle piece between her fingers. "We don't understand why you and Dave don't just make it official."

"And get married?" For no particular reason, my heart began to race.

"No, no. Move in with him."

"We've had this conversation." I was just relieved I had

an already thought-out answer for her. What I didn't have was an answer if Dave happened to ask me to marry him. At least, I didn't think I did.

"I'm well aware," Gran sassed. "I wasn't a fan of your answer then. I was hoping maybe you'd changed it."

"Dave isn't ready to have that sort of talk with the girls," I said, as I'd rehearsed. It wasn't altogether true, but it wasn't a lie either. Dave would be ready—or could be—if I was.

"It's the same reason I don't spend the night," I went on. "I sleep here, you know."

"Sleep is about the only thing you do here. That and laundry."

With a glance around the kitchen, it dawned on me why Gran was acting this way. The table was nothing compared to the sink, stacked high with pots and pans. The house was beginning to take on the appearance it had when I arrived in Creel Creek, near my birthday. It was a mess.

By spending so much time at Dave's house, helping him clean up after the kiddos, watching movies and TV with them, I'd left Gran on her own.

Maybe I do need to spend more time here.

She can clean up herself, Brad's voice came into my mind. *She only acts this way because you let her.*

So, it's not about the cleaning, I thought.

No, it's not. It's about the time.

I know. It keeps slipping—

Don't you dare quote a song lyric!

I smiled, thankful for my familiar's sense of humor and honesty. He knew what was going on here, as he was stuck here most the time. Sometimes, I took him over to Dave's house. But on school nights, he was a distraction to the girls. And Dave wasn't a big fan of his. It didn't help that his thoughts and voice were for witches' ears only.

Then again, Dave wasn't a fan of pets of any kind.

Gran's eyes flitted from the puzzle to my direction. She was probably surprised I hadn't offered a comeback.

"I get it." I was tired of bickering. "I'm free after the harvest festival thing this weekend. We can clean up. And it's the crescent moon this Monday. We'll go up to the graveyard and have a *witching* good time."

"Doubtful," Gran said. "But it'll be nice to get back to a routine, with that crazy business over."

I knew Gran meant murders, but it struck me that perhaps we weren't necessarily over the crazy business hump. "Yeah, well, don't get too comfortable. I just saw Dave."

"How is that news?"

"In the cemetery." I told her about the grave robbery.

Gran pondered this more intently than the puzzle piece she'd held in her hand for going on ten minutes. "I vaguely recall when that happened. They found those bodies in the woods out here, not too far from where they went missing."

"And Steven Robillard?"

"The name is familiar." Recognition crossed Gran's face. "I remember when he died. Not sure they're related."

That was a thought. "Could they be?"

Again, she shrugged. "Are you asking if this Steven fellow was responsible? I told you, I don't know anything about him."

"Right but Dave said the culprit was never found. And this guy died shortly after..."

"If he was the culprit, then why unearth his body now? What good would that do? If you ask me, the same person's responsible. Or it's kids, having a little fun."

"That's what Griffin thought."

"Griffin Barber." Gran made an awful face and shuddered for effect. "There's your culprit right there. That man practically sleeps at that cemetery. He's odd, even for Creel Creek, and that's saying something."

"He seemed clueless," I said.

"They always do. That's how they fool you."

"I'll keep that in mind. I better get going. I promised Dave I'd help cook dinner."

"Lucky man. I never got help."

"No. I just did your cooking for you. Honestly, he does most of it. He's a great home chef."

"And you're a lucky gal," Gran said. And maybe she even meant it.

"All this talk of luck," Stevie put in, "makes me think someone's getting lucky tonight."

"Stevie!" Gran threw the puzzle piece at him. It bounced off his side and fell to the table.

"What? It's what you were implying, was it not?"

"Perhaps." Gran smiled mischievously. Under the table, she waggled her finger in my direction. "Have a good night dear."

I scowled. When she waggled her finger, it meant trouble. Usually for me.

"See you later." I threw open the garage door, passing Gran's dusty Buick on my way to Prongs.

"Crap! Crap! Crap! We went to sleep!" I tore out of bed and struggled to scooch up my jeans, going for the two-legged approach rather than a leg at a time.

Dave squished his eyes closed against a beam of sunlight hitting him square in the face. Another made a bright line across his bare chest, sprinkled with dark hair down to his abdominal muscles, which tightened as he twisted over on his side to avoid the sun's rays.

Saturdays were supposed to be for sleeping in while Trish took the morning shift at Bewitched Books. But this wasn't just any Saturday. And I'd gone and made things worse.

I never slept over at Dave's house. I blamed Gran. That waggle of her finger. She'd magicked this to happen. I was sure.

It had been a typical Friday night. Dave and I cooked dinner—for us, not for the girls. He'd ordered them pizza. Picky eaters don't like grilled pork chops and roasted Brussels sprouts with bacon.

We did the whole routine—the three B's. Baths, books, and bed. They were out by nine or so. After that, Dave and I had the house to ourselves. But we'd stuck mostly to the upstairs bedroom.

Up until now, there'd only been one close call like this—when we'd fallen asleep after binge watching several episodes of *Foodie File Murders* on Netflix. That morning, I'd startled awake around five and rushed out in hopes that Gran and the girls would be none the wiser.

The rising sun announced that our luck had finally run out.

I crept toward the closed bedroom door, listening for any hint of sound from down the hall or downstairs. As I eased the door open, my stomach lurched. The telltale sound of loud commercials reverberated up from the living room. At least one of the girls was up and watching their Saturday morning dose of television.

"It's okay." Dave yawned, stretching his arms over his head. "This was bound to happen eventually."

He kicked off the covers and pulled on a pair of sweatpants.

"But... but I thought I set an alarm."

"You did. You were sleeping like the dead. I had to turn it off."

"Why didn't you wake me?"

He smiled. "I don't want to offend you, but you're kind of grouchy when you haven't had enough sleep."

I glowered at him.

"And you looked so peaceful this morning. I mean, how could I wake an angelic face like that?"

I continued to give him a demon stare. And I know what a demon stare looks like—I've met a couple of demons.

Dave made out like this wasn't as big a deal for him as it was me. Soon, he'd understand. There'd be questions. Questions with answers he wasn't ready to give. The girls were so young. I could never replace their mother, nor was I ready to be their evil stepmother.

This small act—this tiny betrayal—felt like Dave had thrust me into a world I wasn't prepared to face. Granted, I wasn't totally blameless in the matter. I did sleep through the alarm.

"It'll be okay," Dave reiterated. He'd yet to put on a shirt. He brushed past me and allowed gravity to help him down the stairs. Each footfall made the house shake.

Wonderful.

If it had been only one girl, now it was sure to be all three. There'd be no sneaking out this time.

Cautiously, I poked my head around the banister. Allie and Elsie were sprawled on the living room couch together. That meant Kacie, the youngest, was still in bed. I called that a win until Elsie saw my head peeking out.

"Daddy says not to lean on the railing," she scolded.

"That's right. I do," Dave called from the kitchen. "Now, who wants pancakes?"

"Me!"

"Me too!"

"Me three." I shrugged, went down the stairs, and took a seat on the loveseat, opposite the girls.

Elsie hopped over, joining me. Her wide eyes were no longer interested in the show. "Did you have a sleepover without telling us?"

"Guilty."

"Guilty?" She felt out the word. "Like one of daddy's convicts?" She pronounced it long "con" then "vicks" quickly and unsure.

"That's right. They're convicts," Dave emphasized the latter half of the word, "and they're guilty if they've been *convicted* of a crime. It means they did it—like the sleepover."

"I can't pronounce the other word," Elsie said to me, shrugging.

"Perpetrator," Allie announced proudly.

"Well, I'm not one of those," I said, smiling. "And I'm not sure I can pronounce it either. But I am guilty of sleeping over without telling you. I'll definitely let you know next time. I promise."

"When?" she asked. "We can have another sleepover tonight."

This time, Dave did the peeking. He rocked away from the stove, and his eyebrows waggled suggestively.

"No." I shied away. "Not tonight. It won't be for a while, I think. When I'm ready, you'll be the first to know."

Her lips went pouty. So did Dave's.

"Okay," Elsie said. "At least you're here now. We can play."

"That we can. And don't forget, I'm taking you to the fair later while your daddy works. So, get ready for a whole day of fun with Constance."

She smiled her gap-toothed smile then ran to get us some Barbies to play with. They were dressed suspiciously like witches. Out of the three girls, Elsie was my biggest fan.

"Ready?" she asked, handing me a doll.

"Almost," I answered. "I will be. But first, coffee."

Dave brought me a cup, taking a few precious moments away from hovering over his griddle and watching the pancakes bubble. He was a perfectionist—as good at making breakfast as he was everything else.

"Speaking of—" I made a face at Elsie "—what was that word again? Per-pepper-ators?"

"Perp-trators?" she tried then "perpetrators!" she squealed, delighted with herself.

"See! It's not that hard," Allie said, her eyes glued to the TV screen.

Elsie ignored her and held her Barbie up.

I bobbed my Barbie along my leg in Elsie's direction. "I was wondering if anyone had made any headway with the robber from last night..."

"A bank robber?" Elsie whispered as if the mere thought might manifest the villain in the room.

"Not a bank robber." From the kitchen, Dave pointed his spatula at me in mock agitation.

"What? I was trying to be tactful."

"You need to up your *tactful* game." He flipped a pancake. "Honestly, I have to file a report. First thing I'm gonna do when I get in today. I have to head out to the vineyard after that."

"So, you don't think it's anything to worry about?"

"I never said that. But I bet Griffin's right—probably just some kids having fun."

"That doesn't sound like fun to me."

"No, you're right. It doesn't. My luck, it's one of your lot using the corpse for some nefarious deeds. You should ask your Gran about it for me."

"I already did."

"What'd she say?" He popped out of the kitchen with two plates, the first stacked high with pancakes, the other holding a mound of bacon. He had a bottle of maple syrup tucked under his arm. "Girls, your breakfast is served."

I headed for the table, just as excited as the girls were. My stomach growled in anticipation.

Bacon!

Dave pawed a sticky spot on his ribs where the syrup had been. "Your Gran offer any nuggets of wisdom?"

"Not really. She remembered what happened last time and said that guy's name rang a bell but not a very loud one."

"That makes sense." Dave nodded, rationing food on plates. "It was a big story at the time."

The girls slid into chairs. And Kacie, who'd been absent, came sluggishly down the stairs, trailing a blanket behind her.

"Oh, no!" Dave grinned. "It's the bacon monster!"

"Am not!" She was. Kacie had double the bacon of everyone else.

I let the topic go for a while. When we were alone at the table, I finally asked Dave, "What happened to him? Steven Robillard?"

"I'll be tactful," Dave answered, his eyes toward the living room. "It's not a subject for the breakfast table." He whispered, "Suicide."

5

THE LATE HARVEST FESTIVAL

A few hours later, Dave headed off. We'd be seeing him later as he and a few deputies ran security at the harvest festival.

It sort of amazed me that he was okay leaving the girls in my not-so-capable hands. And they were a handful. As soon as Dave was out of sight, they flipped a switch, going from sweet and kind to at each other's throats, arguments breaking out every few minutes.

I was relieved when we finally set off for the festival.

Rather than move booster seats around, I opted to drive Dave's white minivan. I learned firsthand why minivan drivers always act so crazy on the road. The van would barely move unless I pressed the accelerator to the floor. Any time I removed it, it lost momentum instantly, slowing to a sluggish crawl. It was easier just to leave my foot down and hope for the best.

That wasn't the only trouble with the van. The enclosed space amplified the fights. The girls bickered over everything—toys they'd brought along, how many tickets they were going to win at the carnival style games, and the eldest two even argued about which side of the road was better. For the record, it was the passenger side because that's what side had the McDonalds.

I don't make the rules.

I planned to follow Dave's instructions to the letter. I'd already made a huge mistake on Halloween, when I'd taken the girls out trick-or-treating. I put them in danger from a hunter out to kill Dave. We were lucky to return with our lives.

The traffic slowed to a standstill near the vineyard. The cars ahead of us pulled into a cleared-out field, farmland on the Creel Creek side of the vineyard property. A couple of volunteers, decked out in yellow vests with orange traffic wands, waved us through the field, directing us where to park.

Again, I wished we'd taken my Subaru. I didn't trust the minivan's ability to negotiate the churned-up ground. Once the tires came to a full stop, I doubted they'd move again.

"Yippie. We're here!" Kacie jostled her car seat to and fro, unable to unbuckle herself.

"Finally!" Allie moaned. She unbuckled and helped Kacie out.

"Not quite." I scoped out the sizable walk to the festivities, certain I'd be carrying Kacie on my hip at least halfway.

Many miles later, or maybe just a thousand feet or so, we got past the ticket takers and inside the grounds into another cleared field. This was closer to the vineyard, where rows of trellises were plotted neatly up the rolling hill to the winery house. The recently harvested vines were bare.

The house on the hill stood out not for its size, it was modest by today's standards, but because of its gothic architecture. It could easily have played the part of the *Addams Family* home in either the TV show or the movies.

I was hoping the festivities would be closer to it and that I'd see my friend Cyrus. Spotting him in this sea of people seemed unlikely. It was crowded already, and there was a long line of cars waiting at the road.

The games and rides weren't quite as rinky-dink as I'd imagined they'd be. By Creel Creek standards, it was top notch. Cyrus had probably played a part in that. There was a Ferris wheel, a Tilt-A-Whirl, a Funhouse, and even a Gravitron. Each had long and winding lines. So did the food stalls and games interspersed between the main attractions. On the far side of the grounds was the entrance to a corn maze.

It was going to be a long day and it hadn't even started.

Overwhelmed by the people and trying to keep an eye on three girls, I couldn't even search the crowd for Dave. He found us first, waving us over to his post beside the Ferris wheel.

"All right, my lovelies. There's enough tickets here to do about everything twice." He gave the girls a roll each. He handed me some sort of voucher. "This gets you a whole pizza from the concession stand. If you trade it in by two o'clock, we get entered into the grand prize drawing."

"Fancy!" I laughed.

"Don't scoff. It's got about six bottles of wine as well as a free visit to the chiropractor. Each sponsor donated something."

"Well, okay then." I stuffed the voucher in my pocket. It wasn't going to be a problem. I was already starving.

"I'll be around if you need me," he said then squatted and leveled his gaze at the girls. "And you three best be on your best behavior."

"Daddy," Kacie moaned, "you just said best twice."

"That's cause I mean it. Best behavior. That's three times

now. What Constance says goes. And when you're out of tickets, you're done. Finito! So, spend wisely."

"Yes, sir," they said out of sync and without conviction.

In no time flat, they'd breezed through their tickets.

Allie shot ducks with a water gun until she was finally happy with her prize, a stuffed pink duck. Each of the bigger rides cost five tickets and the Ferris wheel ten. They insisted on going, even though I had to cuddle with Kacie in my lap, promising her that it would soon be over. She squeezed her eyes shut the entire time.

Thankfully, they opted out of the other rides and stuck with more age-appropriate games. There was a kid-friendly section of smaller rides I hadn't seen when we entered. The miniature spinning berries tested my stomach's grit. I could barely stomach the pizza after that. The girls ate as I people watched.

Still no Cyrus. But I caught sight of Dave again, helping a woman who'd gotten stuck in the spinning exit of the Funhouse.

At the funnel cakes, I spied another familiar face. Jami Castel was talking animatedly to someone in line. Her curls bounced as she spoke, dark hair gleaming in the sunlight. She wore fashionably round sunglasses and an equally stylish flannel shirt with cuffed jeans rolled above her shoes.

She was careful not to get any powdered sugar on her flannel shirt, but a mist of powder got the better of her, splattering her face and speckling her sunglasses with white dust.

I chuckled a little until Jami moved over enough for me to catch a glimpse of the woman beside her—Summer Shields, the hook-nosed, redheaded reporter from channel seven.

It figured they'd know each other, both being journalists

or whatever Jami was. I wondered if Jami knew about Summer's other pastime. She was half of the podcast duo responsible for holding me and Trish and a few others captive over Halloween weekend.

Not only did Summer have a vendetta against me, but she'd also made it her mission to expose the whole paranormal community to the world.

"Girls," I said. "Where to next? How many tickets do you have left?"

If any...

I hoped to get away without being spotted. Or worse. I didn't want to see Jade, Summer's partner in crime.

Allie counted out individual tickets, one from every pocket of her jeans. "I've got four tickets."

"Kacie has none." I felt bad—I'd used hers for my ride on the Ferris wheel.

"I've got this many." Elsie, who'd obviously been holding out, held up a fistful of tickets. "And I want to do the corn maze."

"You do?"

She nodded energetically.

Yay. More walking.

The corn maze wasn't getting near the amount of love as the other attractions. Only two groups had gone inside since we'd cleaned our table and crossed the grounds to the entrance.

There was a man taking tickets at the entrance. Or I thought it was a man. I thought I'd seen him move. Now, he was stationary, propped against stalks of corn. We drew closer and he sprang up, making the girls jump and my insides as well.

It took me a moment to realize who I was looking at.

"Cyrus?" I let out a full-blown laugh—a guffaw. He was dressed as the Scarecrow from *The Wizard of Oz*.

"In the straw flesh," he said with his slight accent. "Who do we have here?"

"These are Dave's littles. Allie, Elsie, and Kacie."

Acting shy or scared, Kacie ducked behind my leg.

"It's nice to meet you, girls. I'm Cyrus. And this is my cornfield."

"Is it really?"

"It is. I bought this land ages ago." He looked side to side, warily. "I mean my father did." He winked at me.

"I didn't realize this was all yours."

"He," Cyrus said coyly, "meant to expand the grapes over here but never got around to it. I planted the corn this summer. And I laid out the maze myself."

"Is it a tricky maze?" Allie asked him.

"Depends who you're asking. So far, I think everyone's made it out alive."

"That's good." I whispered in his direction, "My legs are killing me."

"I could offer you a cheater's guide—I mean a map—if you'd like. Just in case."

"What do you say girls? Do we need a map?"

Please say we do.

Both Allie and Elsie shook their heads confidently.

"Okay. No map." I sighed. "How many tickets do we owe you?"

"For you gals, it's free. Enjoy!"

I was happy to speak with Cyrus again. It'd been too long. But I wasn't as enthusiastic about his maze construction. After about twenty minutes, the girls were tired. It all looked the same, green cornstalks on both sides of us and dirt path ahead. We got turned around several times and met dead ends twice before Kacie decided she was tired of walking on her own two feet.

"Pick me up?" When she saw my reluctance, she had a better idea. "Put me on your shoulders, and I can see the way."

I wished I'd paid attention while we were on the Ferris wheel—I could've scoped out where the exit was. Or better yet, we could've taken Cyrus up on that map.

Our pace slowed to a crawl, not only because Kacie weighed me down but because the two older girls were indecisive. They were back to bickering, choosing different directions at every fork in the path, with Allie getting her way ninety percent of the time.

Soon, they'd ventured several yards ahead of me. I struggled to keep up. I could barely keep up with their turns.

"Girls!" I called. "Wait up."

At the next turn, Allie heeded my call. Her dark hair swished at the corner of a turn and stayed put. For a moment, I relaxed, then, for no reason, my insides dropped to the floor.

A wave of pure dread washed over me, almost like it had when our trick-or-treating fun morphed into fleeing for our lives.

"Elsie, stop," Allie scolded her little sister. "Constance said to wait."

I made it to the corner to find Allie waiting. But no Elsie.

"Which way did she go?"

"That way, I think."

"You think?" I put Kacie down beside her. "Elsie! Wait for us."

"It's not my job to babysit her." Allie shrugged.

"I know it's not."

"There was a cat," Allie said. "She chased after it. I told her not to."

"Okay." I nodded. "Wait right here. I doubt she got very far."

I took the path that Allie *thought* Elsie took. I went a few paces to find it branch off again. "Elsie?"

No answer.

"Elsie! This isn't funny." I took another turn, found nothing, went back and took the other side for the same result. I didn't know which way to go and was afraid I would forget the way back to the other two girls.

I figured some witchy quick thinking would set things right. I could use my magic to get out of the jam. I muttered a quick spell.

> "Help, help me, please.
> To guide my direction, send the breeze,
> and put my racing heart at ease."

The gust of wind brushed my face, and I was sure that magic was doing me right this time. It didn't suck—not at this moment.

I raced down the path and another gentle breeze blew, directing me down the next turn.

"Elsie? Elsie, where are you?"

The wind swept through the stalks, and I leaned into the turn, confident I'd find Elsie waiting along the path.

Wrong. I found the exit, the end of the maze. I realized my mistake. I hadn't been specific. Magic led me in the right direction, just not to Elsie.

A couple smiled at me, having just finished it themselves.

"Have y'all seen a girl, about yea high?" I gestured to my waist.

They shook their heads. "Sorry."

Huffing, furious that my magic had misunderstood me —or that I had made a mistake—I wheeled around and went back into the maze. Not only did I have to find Elsie, but I had to retrace my steps to Allie and Kacie, too.

It was time I called for backup. I dialed Cyrus's number and breathlessly recounted my predicament.

"It's okay, Constance," he said. "She can't have gotten very far."

"That's what I thought," I huffed. "You don't happen to see Dave around, do you?"

"I don't. But I've got a radio. I'll call him and get everyone available. Honestly, there aren't that many places she could be. You probably just missed her."

"Then why isn't she answering me?"

It was mostly a rhetorical question, but Cyrus answered anyway. "The stalks are like soundproofing. She probably can't hear you."

"That's not reassuring," I said.

"We'll find her. And you go get the other two."

"Okay."

"I'll get Bobo to come around to the exit. Dave and I will split off from here. You, hang tight."

I retraced my steps, trying to remember each turn. *Was it left, left, right, left? Or left, left, left, right?*

As soon as I'd thought the last one, I knew it was wrong. My first inclination had been right, so to speak. Going the opposite direction meant I went right, left, then took the next two rights.

The two girls were exactly where I'd left them.

I'd left them.

My heart sank. The thing I promised Dave I wouldn't do. And I just did it. I was beginning to think I had no maternal instincts whatsoever.

"Hey, girls." I caught my breath. "Let's find Elsie."

I held out my hands for both of them, and we tried another path.

Dave's calls rang out, muffled by the corn. This path went opposite from where Allie had thought Elsie ran off. With two more turns, we found her.

Elsie's eyes went wide as we rounded the corner. She was on her butt in the middle of the path with a black cat curled on her lap. She stroked its back, and it purred softly.

"I named her Licorice," she said.

Dave called again, closer this time.

"Found her," I yelled. I sat down beside her, crisscross applesauce. "Elsie, I told you not to run off like that. We were so worried."

"I wasn't," Allie countered.

"Allie!"

"What? I wasn't."

"Where are you?" Dave's voice was even closer, maybe on the next path, a few rows away.

"Over here!"

The cornstalks shook as Dave cut between them. His head popped out between the stalks.

Elsie hadn't moved, but the cat decided this was the perfect time to make a getaway. It leaped from its cozy spot on her lap and ran up the path.

"Licorice!" Elsie squealed. But it was too late. The cat disappeared into the stalks. The little girl pouted in my direction. "It's your fault, Constance! The kitty got away."

"Elsie," Dave said softly, "what were my rules today?"

"To stay with Constance and be good." She bowed her head and studied her hands in her lap.

"And did you stay with Constance or run off after a cat?"

"The cat." Her chin sunk lower to her chest as she shied away from Dave's gaze.

"And what do I say about cats?"

"They aren't allowed."

"Why?"

"Cause you're a dog person. But we don't have one of those either."

"One day, we will."

"But I want a cat."

"You want a lot of things." He scooped her up into his arms. Her head was still down, her eyes watery, but the hint of a smile flitted across her face. "What do you need to say to Constance?"

"I'm sorry, Constance."

"I'm sorry too," I said. I turned my own wet eyes to Dave, hoping he wasn't mad at me. "Sorry."

"It's not your fault. A little girl running after a cat, a wrong turn, and all hell breaks loose. I told Cyrus he needed spotters in here. You only went and proved my point." He shook his head. "That guy and his arrogance. He's going to get someone hurt... or worse."

6

IN WITCH THE BODIES ARE FOUND

I didn't sleep over at Dave's again that night, not after what happened the previous night. Although I might've slept easier with Elsie under the same roof.

Riddled with guilt, I tossed and turned—so much so that sometime in the middle of the night, Brad scampered off the bed and out of the room. Usually, it was the nocturnal fidgeting of the raccoon that disturbed *my* slumber. The quirks of his host body made it hard for him to keep a humanlike pet schedule. Funny. Every pet I'd had slept like twenty hours a day. But I hadn't had a pet since college.

I found him curled up on Gran's recliner with her other cats. Stevie, on the other hand, was waiting by the food dish.

"Finally, someone's awake," he drawled in his throaty baritone.

I poured food in the bowl. Then, quietly, I poked around to get coffee going.

Aroused by the tinkling of kibble in the dish, Brad trotted into the kitchen. He yawned with an outstretched paw.

"I was basically awake all night, thanks to this one."

Their voices were similar but distinct, Brad's less husky. "No lattes this morning?"

"I've hit my quota for a while. At least until I get the hang of making them."

"A waste of good milk, if you ask me," Stevie said.

"You would think that."

Cats can't shrug, but he managed something similar. Stevie was large for a cat, with feathery black hair and a mane that grayed at the tips. His face looked like a squashed profile of a lion. He wasn't the stereotypical black witch's cat like the one Elsie had chased in the corn maze. He was more regal. And being a familiar, he knew it too.

Familiars are fallen angels, only they didn't fall to hell. They're neutrals in heaven's war, opting out of military service and into the servitude of the mother. Their magic works in the shadow realm, not here on Earth, where they live inside animal hosts. But using their magic, they can protect witches from evil that lurks in the other realms, waiting to surface.

I'd already had a couple run-ins with demons. But there were many other foes hidden in the mysterious realms. Heaven and hell, or something like them, were two amongst the infinite.

A creaking above our heads meant Gran was stirring upstairs. I'd tried to be quiet but the smell of coffee wafting to her room had a rousing effect. She took the stairs slowly, wrapped in a thick robe and sporting her pink bunny slippers.

At the coffeemaker, I took a long, slow sip of coffee, agitating her because she had to wait a whole two seconds for me to hand her the cup that read *Spelling Up Trouble*.

"Well, how'd it go yesterday? Have fun at the fair? Have fun *before* the fair?"

I knew what she was getting at, but she wasn't getting those sordid details.

"It went so good Dave hasn't called me to make any plans today." I told her about the incident at the corn maze.

"Watching children has never been an *easy* job." She sipped her coffee. "And it's only gotten worse in recent years, what with those hummingbird moms."

"You mean helicopter parents?"

"Whatever. They both hover. I don't like helicopters. Notice, you don't see any helicopter feeders in my yard. In fact, if I were to have a second familiar, it'd be a hummingbird."

"I'd love to see that," Stevie said.

"You'd like to eat that," Brad corrected.

"Not like you wouldn't do the same."

"You're both deplorable," Gran said. "Almost like that grave robber. Did Dave catch him yet?"

"Not yet. And get this—he thinks it could be a witch."

"No witch would do such a thing. Even Nell Baker had higher standards. If anything, it's a warlock or a misguided teenager he's after."

"But it's not a teenager if it's the same person as ten years ago."

"I'll give you that—that is, if it is the same person, which I doubt. I wonder what use would they have for corpses? Magic is from the Earth. Once a soul passes on, their life-force goes with them. There's no innate magic left. Nothing but a bag of bones. Now, if they happen to have a soul, well, then that's a whole other matter."

Her words sparked some recognition inside me. "Innate magic," I repeated. "Trish said she's meeting people around town with magic inside them or something like that. Only they don't know it's there."

Gran nodded. "Creel Creek is a strange place, full of strange people. I'm not surprised in the least."

"Do you know what it means to be sensitive to magic? I think that's what she called it."

Before Gran could answer, my phone began to buzz. *Cyrus* lit up on the touchscreen.

She indicated I could take the call and we could continue our conversation later, heading off, coffee in hand, on her way to the living room.

"Cyrus. Hi! I wanted to tell you I'm sorry about yesterday. It was my fault."

"Constance." His voice was distant, like an echo. "Constance, this isn't a social call. I need your help—your immediate help."

"Why? What's up?"

"I've just... I've just stumbled upon two bodies."

The line cut off. And he didn't answer when I tried calling him back.

∽

I HOPED this was why Dave hadn't called me yet—he was busy with an investigation. After all, the sheriff's department was a man—a woman—short. Willow had been on leave for weeks now, and Dave had yet to hire her replacement.

But if he needed my help, why ask Cyrus to call? Why not do it himself?

I got in the car and stepped on the gas, headed for the vineyard, sure that the answers to my questions were a short drive away.

Without knowing where Cyrus had found bodies, I could only guess. Hardly anyone ever ventured inside the vineyard proper. The winery house, where Cyrus lived, was gated and locked.

I remembered the foreboding chill that shivered down my spine in the corn maze. Maybe that had nothing to do with Elsie's disappearance. Maybe I'd found my gift, a sixth sort of sense, not quite a vision into the future like Willow's visions, but a strong premonition.

It was chillier than yesterday. A cold front had swept in overnight. And with it, the morning fog that blanketed Creel Creek. Even on the outskirts of town, the fog had stuck to the ground longer than normal. It added to the ominous setting of the farmland that surrounded the vineyard, and it obscured the vineyard house from view.

The car trundled into the field that had been the parking lot for the festival. It navigated much better than the van. And I parked much closer to the grounds.

Few attractions remained. They were packed up, ready to be hauled to the next location. There were a few campers and trucks in the parking lot but no other vehicles. No sheriff's department SUV either.

I'd guessed wrong. Or so I thought. But a waving hand and a man running my direction from the corn maze said otherwise. I hopped out, jogging, and met Cyrus about halfway.

"Where's Dave?" I asked him.

"I thought you would call him."

I slapped my forehead. "I thought you would. I thought that'd be the first thing you'd do."

He shook his head and looked away. "Dave doesn't trust me. I hoped that if you were here too, that he'd at least give me a chance to explain. The benefit of the doubt."

"You think he would accuse you?"

"He's done so in the past..."

"It was different then. He didn't know you."

"He still doesn't, I'm afraid. You call. And I'll show you what I found."

"I don't think we should tamper with the scene. We should wait for Dave to get here."

"We won't tamper," Cyrus argued. "I just want to show you, so you'll see I had nothing to do with it."

"I already know that."

I wanted to explain to Cyrus that I wasn't some sort of crime scene expert, but he kept walking. And I kept following, struggling to keep up.

Amid the few mysteries I had solved, I'd discovered exactly one body—Eric Caulfield, a vampire and owner of the grocery store—who also happened to be Cyrus's significant other, now in ghost form.

Cyrus slowed and entered the corn maze, and I brandished my phone.

"Where *is* Mr. Caulfield?" I asked.

I tapped on Dave's contact information in my favorites.

"Gathering more evidence for my defense. He's off to try and speak to the deceased."

"And who's that?"

Dave answered the phone before Cyrus could say anything.

"Constance? You there?"

Dave's voice came from my phone. I'd just dropped it to the dirt with a *thud*.

Lying in the exact same spot where I'd found Elsie was the body of Jami Castel. And lying over her was another body, one that looked nowhere near as fresh—a body that looked as if it had already been buried in the ground for a few years or more.

7

IN WITCH WE DISAGREE

For a long time, Dave just stared at the gruesome scene, shaking his head. Absentmindedly, he scratched beneath his ball cap then fixed his gaze on me. "I guess they meant for it to look like Mr. Robillard killed this girl…"

I could tell Dave wanted me to take another peek, but I wasn't having it. I wanted away from this spot, away from the sight of dead bodies. I'd already worked a spell to ward our noses from the stench.

"Mr. Robillard?" asked Deputy Mackenzie, Dave's second in command with Willow gone.

"Steven Robillard," Dave said. "Deceased. He committed suicide about a decade ago."

"His was that grave that got robbed?" Mac was thick in a variety of ways. He filled out his uniform shirt with large muscles and a slight gut. He had short auburn hair—his thick mustache was a much deeper shade of red, the same color as his fur when he shifted into fox form.

"Yes. It was his grave and his body. I guess I get to close that file."

Mac stepped closer to the two bodies to get a better look.

I'd already begged to be allowed to go to my car, but Dave had insisted I stay in case he needed magical help. I wanted to tell him my magical help was unreliable at best and downright counterproductive at its worst.

I stayed.

"I don't see it," Mac finally said.

"Don't see what?"

"How it only *looks* like this guy killed this lady. You ask me, I think he did it."

"He's dead. He's been dead."

"That didn't stop him from walkin' out his grave, did it?"

"There's no such thing as zombies." Dave's head jerked in my direction. "Right? I mean, there's no such thing as zombies?"

I shrugged. "You tell me. I'm not an expert."

He shook his head. "There's no such thing. Whoever did this wanted us to think that's what happened."

"Why would they do that?" The words had come from my mouth. And that wasn't the only betrayal. My eyes went back to the bodies, locked together in some sort of struggle, a mangled and dirty hand wrapped around Jami Castel's neck.

"If I had to guess, they wanted to mess with us." Dave bent down and blocked my view again. "Or throw us off. Or maybe they just wanted to get those podcasters riled up again. Give them another story to tell."

"They wouldn't do—"

"Mac, I swear to you," Dave interrupted him, "if those ladies catch wind of this, it's your head on the chopping block."

Mac winced. "Boss, you could've picked another

phrase." He had seen the bodies of the shifters, all three with their heads chopped clean off.

"All right. How's this? You'll be fired. Is that clear enough?"

"There's plenty other folks who saw this already. You can't hold me responsible."

"I can, and I will. I have it on good authority that you might be Summer Shields' biggest fan. If she catches wind of this, it's on you."

"That's not fair. What can I say? She's cute."

"I didn't say it was fair. Now, go interview those, uh, showmen that are left. Find out if they saw or heard anything last night."

"Showmen?" Mac squinted. "You mean the carnies? Half of 'em skipped town already."

Dave pinched the bridge of his nose. "I've got their names and contact info. I got that information last week when we were setting up. Just talk to who's left. And whatever you do, don't call 'em that to their faces."

"Call 'em what? Carnies?"

Dave closed his eyes and seemed to be fighting off an urge to say something he'd regret. "Yeah. That's the word."

"Don't say carnie," Mac repeated. He headed down the path and disappeared behind a row of corn only to reappear again after realizing he'd made a wrong turn.

"As you can see, I'm still having trouble with that one. And speaking of trouble, how do *you* keep getting involved in stuff like this?"

"I believe you asked me to get involved last time."

"That was last time," Dave said. "Explain to me again why you were here this morning."

"Cyrus called me first. He thought you'd blame him for this."

"And why would I do that?"

"Probably because you blamed him last time?"

"I mean besides that." I went to speak but Dave stopped me, holding up a finger. "Did he and this woman know each other?"

"I think so," I said. "I think Jami Castel was writing something about the vineyard for her magazine. She came through town the other day and stopped at Bewitched Books."

"The coffee girl?"

I nodded.

"This is coffee girl. Not how I pictured her."

"She was a lot less dead the last time I saw her."

"The other day?"

"No." I shook my head, remembering. "Yesterday. She was talking to Summer Shields over by the funnel cakes."

"Speak of the devil." Dave grunted a laugh. "I get to interview her for a change."

"Can you do it without revealing," I cringed and gestured in the direction of Steve Robillard's corpse, "all that?"

"I'll give her the information necessary to conduct the interview. This woman is dead, by way of murder. I need to start learning more about her. A lot more. Find her car and her phone and everything else. While I work on that, do you think you can be of any help here? Can you try to summon a clue?"

"Weren't you just scolding me for being here?"

"Doesn't mean I can't use your help."

"I make no promises." I twirled my finger in the air.

"Fair enough."

And it was a good thing I didn't promise him anything. There was no hum of magic in the air and nothing happened when I tried my summoning spell. Nothing flew into my hand. No word was whispered in my ear. There wasn't even a puff of wind through the corn stalks.

∼

A LITTLE WHILE LATER, Dave allowed me to retreat to the warm comfort of Prongs, and more importantly, well out of view of the dead bodies, while he summoned a small task force to continue their investigation.

Many more vehicles arrived, making the field look like the parking lot it had been the day before. Some were from the Creel Creek Police Department, then an ambulance without its lights on, and behind it, the local medical examiner in her pickup truck.

There were others. Summer Shields, with her cameraman, set up shop outside the police perimeter. Dave hadn't spoken with her yet. She wasn't yet aware of her connection.

Last to arrive was a rusty old black hearse. It pulled in next to the ambulance. I found Griffin Barber's choice of vehicle to be in poor taste. He opened the back to reveal a few shovels and other gear beside what had to be the unearthed casket of Steven Robillard.

Dave went over and spoke to the cemetery's groundskeeper. After, he strolled over to Prongs with his hands in his jacket pockets. I rolled down my window. "Is he really going to pick up that body like it's nothing?"

"Like what's nothing?"

"You know. Like it's not an accessory to murder."

"He isn't taking it to the cemetery. It has to go with the other body to the morgue. We just don't have the vehicles or the manpower right now."

"Still." The horror of it was written on my face.

"Come on, Constance," Dave said. "It's staged. The ME's going to confirm that soon."

"What if she doesn't?"

Dave shook his head, eyeing Griffin, who looked like a fish out of water amongst the officials.

"Need I remind you, Constance Campbell, that you didn't find any magical traces there?" Dave asked. "There's no proof that the body had anything to do with the murder. It's a prop or a gag. Or it's some psychotic's idea of a joke."

Something told me Dave was wrong. That the body was the key to solving the murder—even if it wasn't the killer. And as far as I could tell, it was the only clue. Dave hadn't found Jami's car or her cell phone nearby.

"Need I remind you, Sheriff David Marsters—" two could play the full name game "—this is Creel Creek, Virginia. We don't get the luxury of 'normal' murders." I made air quotes. "Not that any murder is routine."

"Some are," he argued. "It's the boyfriend, the husband, the lover. Heck, it's the stepdad. Even here, in Creel Creek, I've seen my fair share of routine cases."

"I doubt they looked like this."

"You're right, they didn't. But just because it's complicated doesn't mean we're dealing with zombies. I'm not ready to jump to *that* conclusion."

"Okay," I said. "But I have a feeling. A feeling that there's more to this."

"I'm sure there is. There always is."

"Am I allowed to leave?" I put the car in gear, assuming I was.

"You are. I need to formally interview Cyrus. I told him to go back to the winery and wait for me."

"You want a ride?"

He looked up toward the vineyard house, now visible

through the morning haze. The fog had mostly burned off. "Maybe."

"Do you need a chaperone?" I asked, my tone suggesting he did.

"I'm of the opinion I don't. But if Cyrus wants you there, it's fine by me."

"Okay then."

The gate at the road was open. The long drive ended in a circular driveway surrounding a large fountain. A faint mist was hovering over the surface of the nearly freezing water; it shrouded the entrance from view until we walked through it, up the steps to the door.

Cyrus welcomed us into the house himself. I caught a glimpse of his longtime servant Lurque retreating into the kitchen when Cyrus showed us into the house's formal dining room. The room also served as the vineyard's tasting room. There were a number of wines out on display.

Like most of the house, there were touches of Cyrus's upbringing in the decor—objects and ornaments of gold from Egypt, an extravagant chandelier from his time in France, and stored neatly in the corner of the room, a tea set and cutlery fit for an English teatime. There was a large Renaissance-era painting on the wall that Cyrus had acquired during the Renaissance.

"Make yourselves comfortable." Cyrus indicated the chairs at the end of the table. "Would either of you like coffee or tea?"

"A coffee would be great," Dave said.

On cue, Lurque appeared with cups and a carafe of coffee along with a small pitcher of half and half. The portly man with bags under his eyes poured our coffee and left without uttering a word.

"Should I interview him too?" Dave asked no one in particular, maybe me, maybe Cyrus.

Cyrus answered, "If you like. Although he doesn't venture out of the house often."

"When was the last time?"

"Perhaps fifty years ago… if I'm remembering correctly."

"Fifty years?"

"He has a condition, similar to but unlike Eric's."

"Is Eric in the room now?" Dave's eyes darted to and fro above us. He couldn't sense ghosts, not unless they presented themselves to him, but he was wary about Mr. Caulfield's whereabouts all the same.

"No. He isn't back from the shadow realm yet."

Dave tried to hide his discomfort. "He can speak to Constance when he is. I'll make a note of anything he deems important."

"Very well." Cyrus partook in coffee with us, something his anatomy allowed for. "I'm at your disposal, Sheriff. Ask me whatever you like."

Dave set his cup down. "What I'm particularly interested in is why you thought I might blame you—because if I'm being frank, yours was the last name that came to mind, even knowing you were the person who found the bodies."

"I understand my actions were suspicious," Cyrus said. "I panicked this morning. I don't think anyone, even anyone living as long as I have, gets used to the sight of a dead body. It's for that reason I've surrounded myself with those who don't die, people like Eric and Lurque."

"I get it," Dave said. "It's the same reason I haven't had a dog since I was a kid. And why I swore off pets when Becky died."

Dave's wife Becky had died of cancer. He went years

without dating anyone, raising the girls alone. His stance on the cat issue was making a lot more sense now.

"But that doesn't explain everything," Dave went on. "Why were you so worried? Did you know Jami Castel? Or, for that matter, Steven Robillard?"

"I met Jami the other day," Cyrus said. "She came over for an interview."

"Is that it?"

"No." Cyrus checked from one side of the room to another. "I was hoping Eric would be here by now."

"Cyrus, I need you to tell me everything... please."

He nodded. "I will."

"Okay... tell me about the interview."

"It went well. We talked wine. She tasted wine. She wrote down some notes and that was that. She left."

"That's it?" Dave struggled, and I did too.

Why would Cyrus be worried about something like that?

"No," he said again. "She stopped me yesterday at the festival and asked if she could come over for dinner. She had a matter to discuss with me."

"What kind of matter?"

"She figured it out," Cyrus said slowly.

"Figured what out?"

"Me," he said. "She had photos—photos of me, photos of Eric, dating from the vineyard's opening. And others, taken after the first World War. Another, from an article the paper ran in 1963.

"She'd done some digging in the library archives, a great deal of digging actually. I wasn't aware these photos existed. Eric surely didn't know—he had always protected us from this kind of thing.

"And that's not the worst of it... she could see Eric. She knew he was there in the room with us."

"And?"

"What do you think, Sheriff? She threatened us—she threatened to expose us unless..."

"Unless what?"

"Unless we invested in some venture of hers."

"*Virginia Vines Magazine*?" I asked.

"No. Something else. Something like a TV show."

"And what did you say?"

"I was willing to give her what she wanted but Eric refused on principle. I wish he was here to tell you about it—"

"When did she leave?" Dave asked.

"Around ten, I think."

"You're sure she didn't stick around?"

"She departed through the front door. After that, I can't say what she did."

"And when did she plan on exposing you?"

"She never specified. It's possible she already has."

"Possible," Dave said. "And what about this morning? Why were you in the corn maze?"

Cyrus blinked. "It's silly. I wanted to go through it another time. We're supposed to harvest this afternoon. I guess you could say I'm proud of it—too proud."

Dave took a final swallow of coffee, stood, and collected himself. "You've been very helpful. I'll be in touch."

For a moment, Cyrus looked confused. "You aren't going to ask about the other thing?"

Dave arched an eyebrow. "The other thing?"

"Well," Cyrus said, "I am known as the god of the undead..."

"Oh... right."

Dave went to sit down, but I stopped him, holding out my hand. "Wait. Cyrus, I thought that was just a title?"

"Oh, it is. But given the nature of the crime..."

"I see what you mean," Dave said.

"You do?"

"Yeah, you do?" I wore the same perplexed expression as Cyrus.

"Well, I thought I did," he said. Remember how I thought it might be some psycho's idea of a joke?"

"Yeah...?"

"Well, now, I'm sure of it. And I can narrow down the suspect list—because this particular psycho must know Cyrus's secret as well. You, my good sir, were framed."

8

A WITCHING ROUTINE

"Who all knows Cyrus's secret?"

The next morning was a day off for me—the bookstore was closed on Mondays. With Dave working and the girls at school and daycare, I was free to spend my morning torturing Gran with questions.

After a few cups of coffee, I found her in her usual spot in the living room recliner with her feet up. I wasn't allowed to speak—not even during the commercials—as she watched *The Price Is Right* with Stevie curled up on her lap.

Finally, she held up the remote and dramatically smashed the power button. "What was that, dear?"

"Who knows Cyrus's secret?"

She frowned, her typical expression for deep thought—well, thought in general. "Who knows besides us?"

I glowered at her. "That *was* the question."

"I know his secret. You probably think I'm guilty." Gran held out her wrists. "Go ahead, slap the cuffs on me. I did it."

"I should. But no—who else?"

"The other witches do. If I recall correctly, you told them. Agatha, Lauren, Hilda, and—"

"Don't you dare say Kalene!" I countered. "I'm so sorry your usual suspect is no longer here."

"I know. I know. But we've been over this, Constance—a witch doesn't have to be present to cast a spell."

"True. But there wasn't a magical trace like there was with Dad. And a witch would need magic on her side. She'd have to have great need for the spell to work. I don't think Kalene had a need to kill Jami Castel. I don't think they know each other. Not to mention, I trust Kalene and Ivan."

"Not enough to join their fellowship."

"That's not true," I said. "I have a whole list of reasons I'm not ready to join the Faction. Okay, does anyone else know his secret?"

Gran made the slightest shrug with barely any shoulder movement at all. "Some of the shifters may know. Although I doubt they could summon the dead. Their magic isn't powerful enough for that."

"It could've been a familiar," Stevie offered.

"How?" I asked.

The cat licked his paw. At the same time, there was the muffled thumping of paws on the stairs as Brad trudged down. He and daylight did not see eye-to-eye.

"It's within our power to facilitate raising the dead," Stevie said. "It's part of the reason we aren't allowed on sacred ground."

"I didn't know that."

"Think about it, dear." Gran's eyes followed the raccoon as he trotted to the couch and clambered up. "Their power is derived from the shadow realm. Who lives in the shadow realm?"

"Ghosts? Demons? Spirits?"

"All of the above."

"Still," I said, "they'd have to reanimate a corpse—which by the way, Dave doesn't believe happened."

"Dave can believe what he wants. What do you believe?"

"I believe the corpse has something to do with it. Not sure what. But anyway, how would someone, a familiar—anyone really—do such a thing? How would they reanimate it?"

I couldn't tell if Gran was proud or intrigued that my opinion ran so counter to Dave's. She replied, "They find a spirit, and they convince that spirit to come through the portal to earth, likely trapping them here for the rest of their spirit lives, which isn't necessarily eternity.

"That spirit can occupy its former home. It takes a steadfast, or perhaps an obstinate, soul to will their old body back into motion, but it's possible."

"Those are two different words," I pointed out.

"I know they're different words," Gran spat. "It's why I used them both. Steadfast—they're loyal to their summoner. They do as they're told. In this case, maybe they killed that journalist."

"Or they're obstinate." It was a funny word coming from Stevie, the most stubborn familiar of the lot. He continued in his throaty growl, "They come back for the sake of coming back. They never actually wanted to be dead, which no one could blame them for."

"Hmm…" I took this knowledge into consideration. "I have another crazy theory, if you're interested."

"Go on. Let's hear it."

"What if…" I started and stopped. Gran was really going to think this idea was stupid.

"Yes?"

"It's just, I forgot to tell you Jami was sensitive to magic. Or Trish believes she was. I guess now we'll never know."

"Perhaps Mr. Caulfield will find out," Brad said. "Is he back from the shadow realm yet?"

"I haven't heard."

"That's a no," Brad replied. "Cyrus would've sent him over straight away."

He was right. Cyrus had made that promise. And I hadn't heard from him, not from anyone aside from Dave—who believed the other corpse was a prop, no matter how much I argued otherwise.

Granted, we hadn't argued. It wasn't a fight. It was a disagreement. And I hadn't made much of a case for myself, except to tell him I had a feeling.

Then he had the audacity to say something like, "Don't you always have a feeling?"

Well, yes, Dave, I do. And I'm right most of the time.

He was supposed to interview Summer Shields today. They'd yet to find Jami's car or her personal effects after a sweep of the vineyard property and the surrounding area.

"Go on," Gran encouraged. "What's your theory?"

"Oh... it's stupid."

"You already said it's crazy and now it's stupid—"

"Which only makes us want to hear it more," Stevie said.

"All right." I sighed. "What if Jami Castel killed herself?"

"And how would she have done that?" The frown lines around Gran's mouth deepened.

"I don't know. Maybe she wanted to scare Cyrus and it backfired."

"It's certainly a theory," Gran said derisively. "But not a very good one."

"To be fair, I said it was crazy."

And stupid.

"That you did, dear." She feigned a smile, which smoothed out the frown lines.

"Okay then. If it's not a witch or a familiar, not a shifter, not even a hunter, what is it? Who is it? How many other beings are there in this town?"

"A lot," Stevie and Brad said together, their deep voices mingling to make the walls shake.

Gran scowled. "You know, you don't have to get involved this time. You could let Dave get on with his job."

"I know," I said. "And I will. Probably. But Gran, I met her. I met Jami. And even though I don't like what she was doing to Cyrus, I still believe she deserves justice."

"I see." Gran sank back in her chair. "I think maybe I'm with Dave on this one. You've given no evidence for a necromancer in our midst. And there's always the chance a clever resident might've put two and two together."

That rang a bell. "Jade or Summer?" I shook my head. "I don't think so. They're always on my radar for something. And I'm sure they'll cover this on their podcast. But I highly doubt they've murdered anyone."

"You never can tell what someone is capable of," Gran said. "Only that they're capable of something. And that's a lot."

"Is that the case?" I smiled at her. "Tell me, what are you capable of?"

"Right now?" she asked. "A nap. It's bound to be a long night."

∼

I OPTED to get out of the house and let Gran rest up. She was right; it would be a long night. It always was when we had a circle in the graveyard.

The witching hour was just that, the hour starting at midnight. It was one of many factors that could amplify magic. And it happened every night, regardless of if we were witching or not. Mostly, we weren't. Being women over forty, we tended to be in bed asleep.

Another of those factors was sacred ground, hence why we met at a hidden graveyard in the woods. And yet another factor was the moon. Not the full moon, normally associated with werewolves and the like, but the crescent moon, whether it was waxing or waning, that was the most magical in the cycle.

It was waxing now, visible in the cloudless sunlit sky. Our last circle, when we'd gotten our gifts, had been under a waning moon.

I stretched in Gran's front yard. It had warmed up to what I thought of as perfect running weather, the type of weather where shorts and a long sleeve T-shirt made for appropriate attire.

This wasn't going to be a long run and probably not a very fast run either. Gran was right about a few things in regard to my dating Dave. I'd fallen out of my old routines and into something new. I was running a lot less and yet I was more exhausted than ever.

Getting older felt like my new routine. But then, life is made of routines, day after day doing the same thing.

In California, that had meant work. Morning emails. Coffee. Afternoon meetings. Afternoon coffee. Evening emails. Wine. Netflix. Repeat. By the time I was thirty, even weekends of spontaneity—hiking, wine tastings, trips outside the city to Yosemite and the coast—had become few and far between.

My thirties blew past, and it felt like I was never going to catch up. I was never going to live that life I'd always wanted

—that life of freedom and adventure. I was always going to be tied down by something, even if it wasn't kids.

Here in Creel Creek, with Dave and his girls and my new witchy powers, routine had again forced itself on me. I needed to fight back.

But we're all creatures of habit. Take our witchy neighbor, Agatha, for instance. She's out every morning, rain or shine, snow or sleet, in her turquoise track suit, doing laps around the neighborhood.

I waved as we passed each other on opposite sides of the street. She power walked the other way, her arms pumping hard and fast. I veered down her road, cut across someone else's lawn and onto the dirt path along the cemetery fence.

Whatever Griffin Barber thought, I wasn't poking around his cemetery. It was just a nicer stretch of ground without the weeds and brambles by the highway with its highway smells of asphalt and roadkill.

I moved down the chain-link fence at the back of the cemetery and readied for the bend toward the highway. My usual route went the few miles into town, near the city limits to the small park outside the library where the girls liked to play.

This was the last stretch of dirt path ahead of the road. The last easy footing. Soon, I had to take more care. I picked up the pace and sped into the curve, only to find my path blocked.

The road, if it could be called that, was just wide enough for a single car. Like this one. It was parked a few hundred feet from the road and on the other side of the fence from a stone mausoleum—as if someone didn't want it to be seen by either passersby on the road or by Griffin Barber doing his groundskeeping.

I stopped dead. I recognized this car. It was parked in front of Bewitched Books when Jami Castel stopped in.

I pulled out my phone and called Dave.

Five minutes later, Mac arrived. Or he tried to. His cruiser missed the turn, almost hidden from the road. He skidded to a stop, did a wide U-turn, then eased onto the dirt and parked behind the abandoned car.

The broad-shouldered deputy stepped out and waved then struggled into a pair of ill-fitting latex gloves. "I assume you haven't touched anything."

"Nope."

"That's good." Mac made a wide circle of the vehicle, holding up a camera and snapping a few photos.

There wasn't much to see. The car's windows were tinted.

Satisfied with his photos, Mac stepped closer and tried the door. "Locked."

I didn't know what to say, so I didn't say anything. *No one leaves their car unlocked these days.*

He shot me an expectant look. "I said it's locked."

"Okay? I heard you."

"Couldn't you, uh… you know—aloe amora." He gestured like he held a wand and pointed it at the car door.

I couldn't in good conscience give him props for *almost* getting the Harry Potter spell correct. Even if he had, Mac was still on my poo poo list for the way things had gone down at the League Den.

"I'm sure you have a tool for opening car doors," I said.

"Yeah. We do. I just thought magic might be faster."

I made a face. "Doubtful. Since you have a tool, it probably won't work anyway. But I can give it a try."

"That'd be great." He smiled. Part of me thought he just wanted a magic show.

With a simple rhyme—not at all similar to a trademark spell—the locks whirred, and the car's blinkers blinked a couple of times. It worked.

Magic sucks...

"Knew you could do, Hermione." He barely pronounced her name better than Viktor Krum.

"Never call me that again."

Mac shrugged and opened the driver's side door. Without moving, he took a long gander inside. And with him it was definitely a gander. His forehead crinkled in concentration. Finally, he picked up something from the seat and held it up for me to see. A phone. "Looks like I solved the mystery of the missing phone. It's off—that's why we couldn't find it. Now, what other clues do you hold?"

Mac managed to squeeze his shoulders inside the car, hovering over the seat.

"Shouldn't you wait for Dave?"

"I'll have you know, I had training."

"Oh, well, if you've had training..." I couldn't hide the sarcasm in my voice.

But he didn't notice. Or I thought he didn't.

He stepped back, his face more thoughtful than I would have believed if I hadn't seen it. "Actually, maybe not. Maybe we should wait for the forensic folks."

"Why? What's up?"

"Take a peek, if you want—it looks like she's been living in this thing."

Well, I couldn't resist an offer like that.

He was right. Trash littered the floorboards. There were at least a dozen coffee cups from various establishments. Most notable was the generic cup she'd taken from Bewitched Books. It stood out because of its lack of flair compared to the others. Oddly, only a couple were the festive holiday cups from Starbucks. The cups were mixed amongst assorted fast-food bags.

On the passenger seat, she had a stack of folders and notebooks, a couple of composition books, and a planner. They'd spilled from an open saddle bag that also showed a sliver of metallic laptop.

The backseat didn't have any trash, but it fit the motif. A few rocks, fist-size, bigger than a shoe would pick up, were scattered on the floorboard. And there were plenty of shoes calling them neighbors. It was like half a wardrobe in there. The seats were covered with neatly folded clothes and accessories, each thing every bit as stylish as she had been.

"Lotta stuff in there," Mac said.

I nodded. "I'm most interested in those folders and that laptop."

Mac made another face. "Yeah, well, it might take us a while to sift through that information."

I frowned. The way he said it—the us—made it sound like I wasn't included.

9

IN WITCH THE GROUND SINKS

Dave and a few other deputies blocked off the side road. The whole scene was surrounded with crime tape—even into the graveyard, which made sense, given its relationship to the crime.

On the walk back to Gran's house, I spotted Griffin Barber. He was hidden among headstones, spying. I tried to avoid his notice, ducking away behind a hedge, but knew he'd found me when an icy chill ran up and down my spine.

What a creepy guy.

Again, I met Agatha going the opposite direction. She waved.

"See you tonight," I said, waving back.

I made it to Gran's without further incident and with little detail, considering what I'd stumbled upon.

I wondered what Jami had in those folders. Did one contain her evidence against Cyrus? And what about the laptop—they were always a treasure trove of information on crime television—if the investigators managed to unlock them. Like car doors, laptops are almost always locked these days with hard-to-guess passwords.

My dad's password had always been **password** with the O replaced by a zero. *So, so clever, Dad.* I used to sneak on the AOL chatrooms late at night.

Kids these days will never understand.

I came in noisily. Gran was asleep in her chair, snoring lightly, despite my small effort to rouse her. A larger effort would surely put me in her bad graces before our evening stroll up the hill in the graveyard.

And nobody wanted that. Gran was the de facto head of our non-coven. She rejected the idea of covens. In her mind, we were separate witches with our own goals, meeting together to combine our magical strength.

The past few circles ran counter to her stated philosophy. We always had a common goal.

But maybe not tonight...

"What's not tonight?" Brad asked, having read my thoughts.

"Oh, nothing. Just thinking. There's nothing pressing we have to work on together." There'd been so many things to do at these circles.

At my first circle, on my birthday, I was given a few smaller gifts by the other witches, not that I knew how big—or small—my gift from Mother Gaia actually was.

Those gifts were easy. They'd been spoken aloud. I'd been given aid in potion making. Hilda had given me protection against harmful potions—a gift that would irk me for the remainder of the year because it negated the effects of alcohol. And Gran had given me something else, my sort of sixth sense for when danger was approaching.

"What about the murder?" Brad asked.

I shook my head. "I already tried magic. I'm not sure what help the other witches can be."

"I'm sure you'll think of something to do tonight," Brad

said. "You always do. And to their credit, they're usually pretty helpful."

That reminded me. I'd spoken on the phone to Cyrus that morning. "Actually, it's *your* help I need."

Brad straightened. His long, banded tail bristled. "I'm all ears."

"It's in the shadow realm—"

"You already have my help there. Remember? I'm helping sort out that demon nonsense you got yourself into."

"You mean the demon nonsense you got me into?"

"Let's not play the blame game. I was new to this world. You were new to *this* way of life. We both made mistakes."

"Fair enough," I said.

"What kind of help do you need in the shadow realm? And does it take precedence over the other matter?"

"It does," I decided. "It's Mr. Caulfield. He went missing trying to sort out the stuff with this murder."

"You mean he hasn't come back?"

"If that's how you want to word it." I shrugged. "I guess it could be a lot of things. Maybe he's just having trouble finding Jami."

"Maybe."

"But if something is keeping him in the shadow realm, we need to find out why."

"It's a dangerous place for ghosts," Brad said. "For any being, really—if they aren't careful. Then again, the same could be said for this world. You take a risk every single day, stepping out your front door."

I was all too aware of that. And Creel Creek wasn't helping. It was trying its best to be the supernatural equivalent of Cabot Cove from *Murder, She Wrote*.

"So, are you going to help him?"

"It's my job. If you ask it, I'm bound to do it."

"I thought that was only if I demanded it."

"Yeah, well, semantics." He shrugged, something a raccoon is oddly good at. "I'll go poke around."

Brad went on his way, and I was again left to my own devices. One of those being my phone. I poked around on Jami Castel's Facebook page. She had a lot of friends in various places, all of them posting their condolences about her tragic demise. But I didn't find any family—no one who would truly care that she'd died here on her own.

I found the website for *Virginia Vines Magazine* and waded through articles about local wineries. There was nothing yet published about the Late Harvest Festival or Armand Wines, Cyrus's winery.

Another dead end. I was losing interest. When Dave called, he didn't give any new information. He just said that he would be working late, and the girls were staying over at his sister's house. He told me not to worry about them.

Gran woke up midafternoon and I cooked dinner for us. It was close to 11:30 when we began our routine walk out to the graveyard in the woods.

Ever since Summer and Jade happened upon a circle one evening, the graveyard had been hidden behind a well-crafted set of wards. To the casual observer, the trees just went on and on. To us, and in reality, there was a large clearing about two miles from Gran's house. Inside the clearing, there was an iron fence. Inside the fence, and on the level ground, there were several graves, marked by stone headstones that were so worn, most were indecipherable.

A hill rose in the center of the graveyard. Up it, at the top, there was an ancient oak tree, its limbs wider than my hips. Some angled upward to the heavens, others hung down the hill, almost touching the ground. Its limbs were almost bare, but it was covered in moss and lichen.

An owl hooted. My friend was hidden somewhere in the tree. I smiled at the thought.

There, below its branches, the witches waited. Hilda Jefferies, an African American a tad younger than Gran, smiled at us as she whispered something to Agatha, Gran's neighbor. Lauren had made the drive from Charlottesville. She and Trish were having their own conversation.

They stopped talking when Gran neared the foot of the hill. "That just makes me think they're talking about me," Gran muttered under her breath.

"If it makes you feel better," I said, "they probably were."

"Hardy har." Gran struggled to find good footing. The leaves were slippery.

"All right, let's get this party started, ladies," Hilda said. "It's a school night. I'd like to get some sleep."

"What do you have planned?" Agatha asked her, almost like they'd rehearsed it.

"Oh, I've been thinking about a spell to prevent our outside plants from freezing in the winter. I hate bringing them in and blanketing the others. And I don't think anyone would assume magic if we got lazy this year."

"That'd never work," Gran said. "No. Let's put our efforts toward something useful. I could use a hand from everyone here."

"Doing what?" Hilda asked.

"A spell," Gran said, more sarcastic than usual.

"Right. But what does it do?"

"I'll tell you if it works."

Hilda was taken aback. "Jez, I was just asking."

"I know you were. And I told you when I'll answer."

Hilda shook her head, frowning.

"That's not how we do things here," Agatha interjected. "We aren't just going to offer you aid without knowing what you're up to."

"Fine by me," Gran said. "I didn't want *your* help anyway."

"What's that supposed to mean?"

"Nothing."

"I'm tired of this," Agatha said angrily. "You always make out like this is your hill. Last I checked, it isn't named Jezebel Hill. Even if you were first to find it, this graveyard isn't yours. It's for us to share. I'm helping Hilda tonight."

Lauren, her bright blue eyes as wide as ever, raised a hand. "I'd also like to know what the spell does before I offer my hand. Gaia knows what happened last time I did that."

"That's fine, dear. How about you, Trish?"

"I'm afraid I have to toe the party line." Trish shied away, wary of catching Gran's ire.

"Understood." Gran strode closer to the tree. She placed her hand upon the trunk and looked expectantly up at me. "Well?"

"Well, what?"

This was twice in the same day I'd seen that look—and they'd both revolved around the use of my magic.

"Well, are you going to stick your paw on the tree or what?"

"You'll tell me what it's about?"

"In time," she said.

I could feel the others' eyes on me—feel the pressure from them to go against Gran. And I could feel the pressure from Gran to do as she told me to do.

I was torn.

What the others didn't consider was that I lived with Gran. Not to mention, she was my grandmother, my mother's mother. And even though I'd lost my mother early on in life, these last few months, I'd felt so close to her—so close to finding her. Gran had played a big part in that.

"Go on, just do it," Trish whispered.

It was the permission I needed. I shrugged and closed my eyes against Agatha and Hilda's glares, placing my palm on the tree.

There was a momentary surge of power flowing through me into the tree. It mingled with Gran's magic, and came back again, deep inside me.

I could only hope I was doing the right thing.

In my gut, I thought I was. But I had to be mistaken. At that moment, the earth shook and the ground at our feet sank. It sent all of us tumbling down the hill.

10

CREEL CREEK AFTER DARK

EPISODE 77

It's getting late.
Very late.
The creeping dread of tomorrow haunts your dreams.
It's dark out. Are you afraid?
Welcome to Creel Creek After Dark.

Athena: Welcome, everyone—even the trolls and the witches and all you *other* paranormal listeners, you know who you are.

Ivana: More importantly, *we* know who you are. You can't hide.

Athena: I'm your host, Athena Hunter.

Ivana: And I'm Ivana Steak.

Together: This is *Creel Creek After Dark*.

Athena: It's been a crazy week, hasn't it, Ivana?

Ivana: So crazy.

Athena: We should probably explain.

Ivana: That we should.

Athena: What we need to explain is this—we were

supposed to have a special guest on the show this week. A special guest with a special announcement.

Ivana: An extra special announcement that pertained to both her and us.

Athena: Right. Except... I don't even think I can say it.

Ivana: Except our special guest this week was murdered.

Athena: This is not a joke.

Ivana: Far from it.

Athena: We've been going back and forth all week, debating whether to move forward with the announcement.

Ivana: And whether to discuss the murder...

Athena: We've decided to do both. We think our listeners deserve answers—and we want them too. She was our friend and our colleague.

Ivana: As for the announcement, well, she put her blood and sweat into making this happen. We think for it to die at this stage would be a travesty.

Athena: Perhaps now, we should stop speaking cryptically and just come out and say it.

Ivana: Agreed.

Athena: Our friend, Jami Castel, writer, creator, entrepreneur, among many other things, was murdered. Her body was found near the vineyard, here in Creel Creek, Virginia. And paranormal foul play *cannot* be ruled out.

Ivana: The body was found along with another—a body that had recently been taken from the cemetery, dug up after several years in the ground. This was the body of Steven Robillard. Steven took his own life almost a decade ago.

Athena: If you recall, there was some speculation at the time that Steven would never have done such a thing. He didn't leave a note. He had recently bought groceries. There were none of the telltale signs of someone planning such an act.

Ivana: The connection between the two people, if there is one, is unknown.

Athena: I just can't believe she's gone. She was so excited to share her story with you all today. In fact, she wouldn't even give us a hint as to what she was going to say—only that it was big news.

Ivana: Which brings us to *our* big news.

Athena: We love podcasting. We love for our voices to be heard. And with After Dark Con, we got to thinking… it was a lot of fun for the audience to see our faces.

Ivana: We teamed up with Jami to create an all-new experience for you folks. Starting with the next show, you'll be able to see our faces too. We're going live.

Athena: And that's not it! We're inviting you to create with us.

Ivana: Sign up.

Athena: Find us.

Ivana: And start streaming…

Together: On ParaTube!

Athena: The site is live as we speak. We can't wait to meet you there.

11

IN WITCH WE DISAGREE... AGAIN

"That's it?" Dave asked.

"That's it," I said. "That's what happened."

"And none of you got hurt?"

"No. No one was hurt. Not even Gran's pride."

"So, even after everything, she wouldn't tell y'all what she was up to with that spell?"

"She made it out like it was nothing—like miniature earthquakes are normal. They happen all the time."

"That's crazy."

Dave had his hands in the sink, washing the pots he'd used for the spaghetti. His diet catered to the girls' tastes. Picky eaters—they liked two, maybe three dishes, tops. Spaghetti, chicken Alfredo sans chicken, and chicken tenders—made up of unknown chicken parts, usually shaped like dinosaurs—those were their favorites.

If Dave wanted anything for himself, something like a steak or a burger, he was forced to make two meals. In a pinch, they'd eat macaroni and cheese or grilled cheese, really almost anything with cheese. We'd taken the easy route tonight.

"It *is* crazy," I agreed. "Now, I'm more interested in knowing if you fired Mac."

"Why would I fire Mac?" Dave cocked his head and set the bread pan on the drying rack. He grabbed the next pot without looking.

"Uh, I listened to the latest episode of *Creel Creek After Dark* this afternoon. And someone definitely tipped Summer off about the bodies."

Dave put the soapy pot down in the sink. He twisted, folded his arms, and rested on the counter to face me. "About that…"

I raised an eyebrow.

"Yeah. That was actually me," he said. "I wish I knew how she does it, or rather, did it. Summer flipped that interview like a coin. I told her everything—almost everything. And I barely got anything from her except…"

"Except what?"

Dave shook his head, not meeting my gaze.

"What?"

"Constance," he said with a hint of irritation in his tone, "this is a police matter. Didn't we already agree there wasn't any funny business going on?"

"You mean magic, right? Cause from where I'm standing, there was *a lot* of funny business."

"That's what I meant. No magic. No hunters or anything like that. At least none that I'm aware of."

"So, I'm only any use to you if there's magic afoot? Any other weirdness and I have to hear it on the local news or worse, the podcast?"

"She's not at liberty to talk about it… not yet."

"Dave…"

He scrubbed his face with a hand. "Constance, what do you want me to say?"

"This is what Mac was talking about—this is what he meant when he said it might take a while for *us* to sift through Jami's stuff. He was trying to say, more tactfully than you're accomplishing, that you're cutting me out of the investigation."

"Mac wasn't supposed to tell you anything," Dave said.

"He didn't. It was what he didn't say."

My temper was rising, a rare thing around Dave Marsters, who usually relaxed every inch of me with a touch of his hand or a smile.

I closed my eyes. "Mac not telling me something and you not telling me something are two very different things."

"It's *my* job, Constance. It's my job to find and arrest the bad guys. It's not yours."

"You're serious? You don't think I know that?"

"I can see you're mad."

"You're so observant," I snapped.

I shouldn't have been so offended by this. He was right. It was his job, not mine. But I'd helped in other investigations. To be shut out of the case by my own boyfriend felt wrong... even if he was in the right.

"Constance..."

It was my turn to play the strong silent type. The only sounds came from the television in the living room—the girls watching their nightly ration.

Dave pinched the bridge of his nose. "Can we agree that if I tell you something, you aren't going to do anything about it? You aren't going out sleuthing on your own?"

"I never mean to sleuth on my own," I said, defensive.

"Promise me you won't."

"I promise... just tell me."

"Okay. I will. There was something funny on her phone. She got a message, but not in the message app—it was some other app. The text came right after she left the vineyard that night. It said, 'Meet me in an hour.' We think it was from the killer."

"But you can't tell who it's from?"

"No, it's got some sort of weird encryption. It's a special sort of app."

"Okay." I thought about offering my help, thinking I might recognize it, but I was pushing my luck already. "And what did you hear from Summer?"

He sighed, conceding to answer me again. "She said that Jami was happy about something when they met at the festival."

"Happy about what?"

He sighed again. "I knew you were going to worm this out of me eventually. Honestly, I thought it would take a little longer."

"I'm that good," I said. "What was she happy about?"

"Something to do with a guy—her boyfriend, I guess."

"Her boyfriend?" I asked, somewhat surprised by this new information. But I shouldn't have been. Boyfriends, husbands—they're always the prime suspects.

"Yeah... her married boyfriend."

"Oh...that's two suspects then?"

"Maybe." He nodded. "Maybe it was a crime of passion. After all, she was throttled to death—she let them get in close. So, the boyfriend could definitely have done it."

I put the pieces together in my head, and like a jigsaw puzzle at a vacation house, it was missing some. "No, that doesn't work."

"You don't think?"

"I mean, maybe... but no."

"Why not?" he asked.

"Let me think, aside from the fact that the grave was robbed ahead of the murder? It had to be premeditated."

"Maybe." He shrugged. "Maybe not."

"No. Why would either the boyfriend or his wife dig up a long-dead body and keep it laying around to frame Cyrus? And why move her body?"

"Why do you say it was moved?"

"Because her car was over by the cemetery."

"Well, he was likely planning on breaking up with her, wasn't he? And killing her, for whatever reason. So, he planned that out too—the digging up of the body and moving both of them."

"Seriously?" I scrunched my eyebrows together about as close as they'd go. "That's more crackpot than my zombie theory. Dave, please tell me you're a better detective than you're letting on."

He grinned. "Fine. I'll level with you. I was kind of hoping you'd take that bait. I don't think it's the boyfriend or his wife. But I have to check those boxes and run down their stories."

"You already talked to them?"

He nodded.

"And?"

"And neither knew anything about Cyrus. The boyfriend couldn't have done it. He has an alibi."

"And her?"

"No real alibi but nothing that puts her at the scene either. And supposedly, she didn't know about the affair... not until..."

"When?" My eyes went wide. "Wait... seriously? Not until *you* talked to her? He didn't tell her?"

Dave shook his head.

"Just because he didn't tell her doesn't mean she didn't know." I had my own experience with cheating spouses.

"Right. She *could've* been acting. But like I said, there's nothing that puts her near the scene."

"Okay. So, it wasn't either of them or Cyrus. Who *do* you think it was?"

"Someone else," he said coyly. "Jami could've been running this game on someone else too. That's where my money is. She tried to blackmail the wrong person. And maybe that person knew she was trying to do the same to Cyrus."

"That's a much better theory."

"Thank you. It's why they pay me hardly any bucks."

I smiled and stepped closer to him. He held out his hands and I took them. They were rough and still damp from the dishes.

"Yeah. Yeah. You like me now, cause you got your way."

"Thank you for the info."

"Info you aren't going to do anything with, right?"

"Why would I?"

"You'll tell me if you have some sort of eureka moment, right? You promised no sleuthing. I'm going to hold you to it."

"I promise." I squeezed his hands. "Thanks again for dinner."

"You aren't staying again... are you?" His face fell.

"I'm not."

"Promise me it's not because of this fight."

"No," I said. "The fight's over."

"You're still mad about the other day?"

I gave him a peck on the lips in answer. But that was as far as it was going. No matter what, there wasn't going to be a repeat. "Your punishment will be over next week."

He made puppy dog eyes, nowhere near as cute as his girls'. "That reminds me... next week's plans have changed."

My brain struggled to find his meaning.

What's happening next week? I'm going to work. I'm going to learn marketing and try to start selling coffee.

He squinted like he couldn't believe I was lost.

Oh, right. It's November.

"Thanksgiving? I thought I was going with you to Imogene's."

"That's the thing," he said. "She realized she's having her in-laws over this year."

"She just realized?"

"Oh, Jared says he mentioned it. Knowing him..."

"He didn't," I confirmed. "Until he did."

My insides squirmed a little at this talk. Funny enough, I'd rather be talking a murder investigation. Thanksgiving just wasn't my holiday. I felt like a tagalong.

When my father was alive, we hardly ever made a big deal out of it, opting instead to be together at Christmas. There were a few times I went with Mark to his family's get togethers where I sat on the sidelines—literally—as he and his cousins played their annual game of tag football.

Our last Thanksgiving together I spent working while he was gone. I ordered takeout that night and binged on Christmas movies. In my mind, of the two holidays, Christmas reigned.

I'd already been contemplating the girls' gifts. Thanksgiving was just a bump in the road.

"So, packed house, huh?" I said. "Am I uninvited?"

"Nothing like that. We're invited. You're definitely invited."

"I feel a but coming on."

"Well, I got to thinking. I wasn't sure if your Gran had any plans."

Right... Gran. In my self-pity, I'd forgotten her. "I doubt Gran has any plans for Thanksgiving."

"I don't feel right depriving her of you on such a special day," Dave said. "That's why I offered to host everyone over here. You can invite Gran and Trish. Whoever you want, really. They're all welcome."

"You're serious?"

"Always."

"Dave." My hand found his cheek. He could be so thoughtful. "That sounds great."

He kissed me then drew away. "Does that mean you're inviting them? I only ask because I've got to make enough for everyone."

"Can I help?"

He smiled, the first genuine smile since our argument. "I was hoping you'd ask..."

12

THANKSGIVING

There were few updates about Jami Castel's murder over the next few days.

The girls were off that week for the holiday, staying with Imogene during the day when Dave was at work. But I took them on Wednesday. They were my little helpers at the store. Mostly, that meant helping Twinkie get into mischief of one kind or another while I packed up boxes for witches across the country and around the world.

We closed early—it was still light outside—and headed for the grocery store. Dave had given me the list of things he needed for Thanksgiving dinner. The menu included the normal fare, a ham and a turkey, green bean casserole, yeast rolls, and cranberry sauce. He planned to make creamed corn with fresh corn from Cyrus's maze. He'd already made several kinds of pie.

I had some concerns about his method for cooking turkey. He set up a fryer in the back yard.

"I thought we could put the picnic tables together in the garage and all eat together. No kids' table this year. No one eating alone at the kitchen sink. And most importantly,

Jared won't get crumbs on my couch while he's watching football."

"Sounds like a plan," I said.

But there were three girls with differing opinions.

"In the garage?" Allie moaned. "Dad, that's a dumb plan."

"Yeah, so dumb." Elsie's eyes fixed on the garage door and never left it.

Kacie stood in the center of the kitchen shaking her head, her lips pouty. She didn't say a word, which wasn't like her.

"Are y'all really calling my plan dumb?" Dave laughed. "What's gotten into you three?"

"Nothing," the older two said far too quickly. Kacie held her mouth closed. Her eyes were still glued on the door to the garage.

Dave shot me a questioning look.

"Don't ask me."

It was easy to see they were up to something, only neither of us knew what. Given the way Elsie, and now Kacie, stared at the garage door, I figured I could find out.

And I could do it without giving anything away to Dave until I knew what they were up to.

"How about I take the girls into the garage and they explain why it's not such a good idea?"

"I can come—"

"No." My voice joined their chorus.

"I've got this," I said. "You get that turkey going. And don't burn the house down."

"You're sure? I don't mind taking a few minutes to—"

I scooted closer to Dave and whispered in his ear, "I think they're hiding your Christmas present in there."

"Oh... oh." He nodded. "Right. I'll get the fryer ready."

It was much too early for little girls to worry about Christmas presents for their dad. But he didn't need to know that. My heart lurched as I realized facilitating that was probably my jurisdiction. As long as I wasn't stepping on Imogene's toes.

Who am I kidding? She has enough on her plate. Of course I can take over.

Plus, I had to think of my own gift for Dave—not an easy task. Significant other gifts fall into two categories: easy but inappropriate or thoughtful and something they'll probably never use.

Easy—something lacy. Or thoughtful, my preference. But Dave, being a man of a certain age, was prone to go out and buy whatever he wanted or needed. I had to be thoughtful enough to get something he would never think of—which is probably the true definition of thoughtful.

The girls followed me into the garage. "Okay," I said. "What's going on out here?"

"Nothing." Allie fiddled with her bike, parked in a row with a few others.

"We just don't want to eat out here. It's gross."

"Oh, that's it then?" I studied each of their cute round faces. Elsie tried her best to look me in the eyes and nod, but something behind me caught her attention.

I started to turn, but she grabbed my wrists with both hands. "Constance, please don't tell."

"What are you hiding?"

A black cat darted under Dave's tool chest. The cat from the corn maze.

"She must've followed us home," Allie said.

"She likes it in here." Elsie tiptoed over to the tool chest, holding out her hand. "Here Licorice. Psst. Psst."

"Girls, you know your dad comes in here, right?"

"Not as often as he used to," Allie contested. "Not since he started kissing you."

"But he's going to find the cat. How long has she been out here?"

"We found her last night," Elsie said. "Right after we got home from shopping. She was in the back yard!"

"And you've managed to keep her a secret a whole twelve hours. I'm impressed."

"We only have to keep her secret for a little while longer." Allie stooped beside Elsie. Hesitantly, the cat crawled out and onto Elsie's lap, accepting the love of both girls.

It grew wary when Kacie skipped over.

"Why's that?"

"We have a plan," Allie said.

Elsie nodded. "I'm asking Santa for a kitten. And even if he doesn't bring me one, we can pretend like he did. Daddy doesn't have to know."

There was a minor flaw in her logic I couldn't point out.

"She's good at hiding," Elsie continued. "I think she knows he doesn't like her."

"He doesn't like any cats." Allie stood up again. "But if we eat in here today, he's sure to find her. Unless... unless you've got a better idea, Constance?"

"What makes you think I would have a better idea? What makes you think I'd want to help you? I should tell your dad right now."

"No!" they said in unison.

I motioned to quiet them. No use having Dave rush out here and find it. I wanted to talk it through. Dave didn't have a real reason for his no pet rule. He wasn't allergic. He was just scared—scared of loving something and watching it grow old. If he was willing to take a chance on dating me, of allowing me into the girls' lives, he could do the same for a pet.

"Okay... okay... I'll help. But after today, we've got to figure this out. You can't just hide a cat under your dad's nose."

Allie made a face.

"What is it?"

"His nose."

Right. Their father was a werewolf. It was a wonder he hadn't already sniffed her out.

"We were hoping you might do a spell," she said.

"A spell? Really? To mask the scent? Where is she going to use the bathroom?"

"In the sandbox over there." Elsie pointed to the corner of the garage. "We don't play with it anymore."

"I play with it," Kacie whined.

"Not anymore, you don't. Gross."

"Can the spell be for sound too?" Allie asked. "She can be kind of loud."

"Girls... there's no way we're getting away with this. He's going to notice eventually."

"Just for today, then." Elsie's eyes did that puppy dog thing—something a cat could never get away.

"We tell him tomorrow?" I asked them.

They all nodded, the pretty little liars, smiling like they'd really gotten away with something.

I hastily rattled out a spell.

"Dave," I said. He'd already got the bird frying in the backyard. "I think the living room might be a better idea."

"The living room?" He scowled and pursed his lips. "Are you sure? The kids might spill on the carpet. And Jared's bound to. He's worse than any of them."

"We could try out here, but it's kind of cold."

Dave pursed his lips. "No, you're right. I guess the living room is fine. I'll bring the tables inside in a minute."

"You know," I smiled, "I think I've got it."

∽

A LITTLE AFTER NOON, the guests began to arrive. That was another thing I didn't like about Thanksgiving. Neither the people nor the food were punctual. It was another thirty minutes before everyone was there and took another twenty before the food was ready.

It was a good thing we'd had a decent breakfast. Otherwise, I might've put my magic to use, forcing bread to rise and adding an extra couple of burners to an already overloaded stovetop.

Trish brought Gran for me. And Gran brought homemade mashed potatoes. She settled in at the end of the table, next to Imogene, Jared, and his parents. "It's been a while since I made anything special for Thanksgiving," she said. "And even longer since I've seen such a feast."

"We're glad you could make it," Dave told her.

The kids took over the center of the table, leaving Trish, Dave, and me on the end closest to the TV. A football game played on mute, and every now and then, Jared craned his neck in our direction for the score.

It was hard to hear over the children, but we made polite conversation, the three of us.

"So, Trish, it's been a while," Dave said. "How are things? You keeping Constance in line?"

"No, we hardly see each other," she said. "In fact, I haven't been to the bookstore this week. The Wednesday before Thanksgiving is pretty much the grocery store equivalent to the Super Bowl."

"I can see that."

"I'm beat." Trish sighed. "It was a nightmare. We had all four checkout lanes open."

"I thought there were five lanes." I pictured the layout of the grocery store in my head. I'd worked there for several weeks, then I was fired by Jade for no reason whatsoever.

"The register at lane five has been broken as long as I've been there. But we really could've used it yesterday—could've used an extra pair of hands too."

"Not these hands." I held mine up. "Jade made that pretty clear."

"Yeah, well, I swear, she's only keeping me around through the holidays. I'll be fired too—and our coffee sales will have to pay my rent."

"Oh, it's *our* coffee sales now, is it?"

She shrugged. "Last I checked, I'm the best barista we got. Oh, but you'll never guess who came through my line yesterday."

"Summer Shields," I guessed, and I knew I was right. Creel Creek is a very small town.

Trish nodded and was about to speak when Dave interrupted through a mouthful of creamed corn. "Why is it when people say you'll never guess, it makes guessing easier?"

"I don't think it makes it easier," Trish countered. "I didn't want her to try. And I haven't told y'all the significance of it."

"I'll guess this time." Dave straightened, puffing out his chest in a theatrical fashion. He gripped the stem of his wine glass and held it up, as if to get our attention. "The local reporter, Summer Shields, bought a Tofurkey. She's become vegetarian for Thanksgiving."

Trish rolled her eyes. "Let's, uh, not."

"Oh, no, that's not it?" Dave clearly couldn't sense Trish's agitation. "I know! She bought a bag of potatoes, a ham, and three cans of cranberry sauce."

"How much wine have you had?" I asked him.

"Too much." Imogene poked her head above the children.

He swirled the half full glass but didn't take another sip. "Sorry," he told Trish. "You were saying?"

Trish had deflated. Whatever she was going to say wasn't a joke. Not that Dave's jokes had been particularly funny.

"She's sensitive," Trish finally stammered.

"Who—who's sensitive?" Gran just now caught the conversation at our end of the table.

"Sensitive to what?" Imogene asked.

"To magic," I mouthed.

Trish made a face like there was a terrible smell. And there wasn't. The table was full of deliciousness.

"Wait, what?" Dave asked.

"Who's sensitive to magic?" Gran put a hand to her ear.

"Summer Shields," I said loudly. "She's part witch or something. She just turned forty the other day."

Dave's glass clinked down on the table. Wine raced across the tablecloth and down to the floor. And he didn't even rush to clean it up.

13

CREEL CREEK AFTER DARK
EPISODE 78

It's getting late.
Very late.
The creeping dread of tomorrow haunts your dreams.
It's dark out. Are you afraid?
Welcome to Creel Creek After Dark.

Athena: Welcome to a new era of *Creel Creek After Dark*. I'm your host, Athena Hunter.

Ivana: And I'm the excited Ivana Steak. Welcome to a special Thanksgiving episode of the show. A truly epic episode—a first of its kind, really.

Athena: I'm not sure that's accurate. To me, this is like a midnight matinee mixed with a gritty true crime docuseries.

Ivana: So, uh, something totally new?

Athena: Ha! You've got me there. But listeners can still find the podcast on our website and everywhere else podcasts stream.

Ivana: True. Nothing has changed there. We'll be delivering content in that form for some time. But...

Athena: But you can now find us—and see our smiling faces—on ParaTube, an all-new content sharing service where you can upload or stream content related to the paranormal.

Ivana: Speaking of smiling faces, Athena, I'm happy you're smiling again. The past few weeks have been kind of rough.

Athena: I know. I know. But I've officially put an end to my pity party.

Ivana: Why's that?

Athena: Besides the fact that it was putting a damper on the show and my private life?

Ivana: Yeah... besides those valid reasons.

Athena: Well, I'll tell you why. I admit After Dark Con dealt me my lowest blow ever—professionally or otherwise. I had to take a hard look at the woman in the mirror. Not only at her but at the show and Creel Creek in general.

Ivana: Okay...

Athena: We've been known to stretch the truth—or rather, to speculate about it. And sure, we've dug in deep on some conspiracy theories. But never once have we lied to our audience. It's that accusation that stung me the most. I'm tired of lies. I'm tired of everything that happens in this town getting swept under the rug.

Ivana: Me too.

Athena: Take, for instance, Jami's murder. It's been days and what? Nothing's happened.

Ivana: I've noticed. It's like no one even cares. The whole town turned a blind eye to these recent atrocities. It's like they're under a spell.

Athena: They probably are. Us too.

Ivana: But...

Athena: How did you know there was a but?

Ivana: The script. But also, you've got that look about you. And see, another smile.

Athena: You're right. I am smiling. Because I know this—I know that Jami was working on something special, something she meant to share here on ParaTube with everyone. And it was almost ready.

Ivana: But she didn't leave it for us—and we can't seem to find it...

Athena: Minor details, Ivana. I'm sure we can find it. I only worry whether *they* let us...

Ivana: By they, I'm guessing you mean the witches?

Athena: No. Actually, I meant whoever killed her. I assume it's related.

Ivana: Ah, well, them too. Eek!

Athena: What? A cold-blooded killer never stopped us before.

Ivana: True. So, what's the plan? I'm guessing you have a plan.

Athena: I always do, Ivana. It's time we do what we do best. We gather the facts. We dig up the dirt. And we scoop whoever stands in our way.

Ivana: And the witches?

Athena: We don't play by their rules anymore. It's our game. Our rules.

Ivana: Well, that certainly has piqued my interest.

Athena: Good. Then you're ready?

Ivana: For what?

Athena: To get into a little mischief... 'cause, guess what? I know exactly where we should start.

14

PEACE TALKS

I hated working alone in the bookstore, but not for the reasons people might think. I could handle the isolation—the actual being alone part when the store was quiet, lacking anyone but a familiar or two.

Those were the times I read. I listened to books. Podcasts, some good ones, and one not very good at all.

Trish was happy as long as I got the orders out in a timely manner.

No. What I hated most was when customers did decide to show up. I felt trapped in there with them, with no backup to speak of, except for a mouse or a raccoon. Today, they were both in the shadow realm, looking for Mr. Caulfield. So, there was no backup at all.

It was so much easier with Trish around. She had the right to be rude, to refuse service, to ask customers to leave. It was her store after all. She could do whatever she wanted to whomever she wanted.

I, on the other hand, felt the need to be polite.

Usually, that came easy to me. But there were always exceptions.

The last time I'd truly been uncomfortable managing the store by myself was when Ivan Rush appeared, attempting to recruit me for an organization known as the Faction. I'd sort of hyped them up in my head after learning they had a hand in my mother's disappearance. To me, they were the Freemasons and the Illuminati mixed with the mystery of Atlantis.

Only I found out that Ivan was the Faction's sole member. Everyone else was lost. He kept a register of names, all of them scribbled out. Now that Kalene had joined him, there were two official members and three names on his register—mine being the third.

Ivan wasn't nearly as bad as I'd thought that day. Misguided, yes, but not a bad person. I'd just gotten a text from him.

Constance, it's crazy out west. Like it's Wild Wild West—and I don't mean that Will Smith movie. We had to take care of a vampire last night.

Get this... The shifters here, they're afraid. They don't trust us. We could really use your help.
Another name just appeared in the book. Portland, Oregon—go figure. We plan to head there next. Any chance we could meet up?

As much as he'd like to believe I was a part of his group, I'd never agreed to it. And I would continue to refuse the offer. That made four names in the register.

And no chance, Ivan.

I'd text him the reply if I wasn't so busy... it being Black Friday and all.

Ha!

Not that Bewitched Books partook in such festivities.

There were no special sales. And even more important than that, we didn't open at the crack of dawn.

The empty storefront mocked me.

As if by magic, the door chimed. It startled me out of my head cloud. I put my phone beside the register to at least give the appearance that I was working.

To be fair, I wasn't planning on using it. I probably wouldn't text Ivan again for the rest of the year, if I could help it.

As it was, the customer barely acknowledged me. She was the same here as on the street in our neighborhood. But I'd probably be in trouble if I failed to acknowledge her. "Oh! Hi, Agatha. What brings you in today?"

Agatha Sundwick was older and silver-haired, hair she wore in a tight bun. Unlike Gran, who kept her aging Buick in the garage and herself in the house, Agatha was an active lady. In addition to her morning walks, Agatha was active in the community—she volunteered at the hospital and sang in her church choir. And she was an active witch, one of the few customers who bought and traded magic books regularly.

"I'm looking for a potion," she said. "Something for my cat."

"Something for your familiar?"

Agatha straightened. "My cat. I don't have a familiar."

That was good. Cats and familiars are whole other beasts. Even if they happened to look identical, they weren't. And as far as I knew, familiars couldn't get sick.

"Oh, I'm sorry. I didn't know."

"Not all witches are as lucky as you," Agatha said. "Some of us have to go about things on our own."

I hadn't meant to offend her. I knew familiars weren't always in the cards. Kalene didn't have a familiar either.

"Let's see. We have *1001 Potions and Remedies for Common Pets*. Other than that, I'd have to do a search. Or, I guess, you could try a summoning spell."

"I could?" She glared at me. "Don't you mean *you* could?"

Another thing about Agatha was her temperament. She and Gran had a long-standing feud, probably over how high the other clipped their hedges—Gran being the kind of person who wouldn't clip her hedges at all. And the other night in the graveyard had gone and made things worse.

In fact, I realized now that was probably why she was here in the first place. She wanted to get something out of me. "Gran wouldn't tell me about that thing the other night," I said. "She still won't. I'm sorry."

Agatha's eyes narrowed. "I don't remember asking you about that. I asked why on earth I'd need to do the summoning. It's your store. Or rather, you work here."

Okay, maybe I was wrong.

"I could try."

"Your magic's acting up again, isn't it? It was probably that spell your Gran put on you. I got a grass stain on my skirt, you know. All your Gran's fault."

So I'd been right.

"I'm not sure it was that spell," I said. "And again, Gran hasn't told me what that was about."

"You're too trusting, dear. And your Gran is as sly as a fox."

"Right on both accounts."

We stood there a moment in silence.

"Well, are you going to summon the book or what?"

"I... I'll try it."

"Don't let me inconvenience you," she said, but it

seemed like that was what she was there to do. "I saw you're busy, playing on your phone and the like."

"I wasn't—" I shook my head and bit my tongue—but not literally. It wasn't worth an argument. This was one of those times I wanted to speak my mind, and Trish definitely would have. But I held back and coughed out a rhyme,

> "A book for a cat, under the weather,
> a book with a spell to make the cat better."

I opened my hand, ready for a book to fly off the shelf and rocket into it.

Nothing happened.

"Maybe it's your rhymes, girl. They could use some work."

"Gran says it's not the rhyme that matters. It's the intent."

"She *would* say that. She a terrible rhymer. Fine. I'll give it a go."

> "Counting one, two, three.
> I need the book that's best for me.
> Four, five, six.
> There is no simple fix.
> Seven, eight, nine.
> For a cat, so divine.
> Counting to ten…
> I summon the book within."

We waited. But again, nothing happened.

"I guess it's not here," she admitted. "I'll take that 1001 Potions book."

I summoned it without even a rhyme.

"See, intent." I beamed. And I wondered if she always counted like that. To me, that seemed like cheating.

Content, or appeased anyway, Agatha spun on her heel with her book and headed for the door. That was one uncomfortable encounter over with.

But another came straight in. In fact, they bumped into Agatha at the door, almost sending her tumbling backward.

"Sorry, we didn't see you there," said a familiar voice.

This was worse than Agatha Sundwick. Much worse.

Summer Shields, the owner of the voice, strode inside with Jade Gerwig at her hip. They both sneered at the sight of me. Granted, my face mirrored theirs. But there was something else. The way they held themselves, there was a sort of confidence, something they rarely showed around Trish.

But since it was just me here...

That trapped feeling I'd been having was amplified to eleven. My back was against the wall, and I couldn't escape through the back room.

Could I?

It was all I wanted to do—get away. Get as far away from these two women as possible and live to fight another day.

Not that I was scared of confrontation. Trish would be a hundred percent on my side in these circumstances. Magic would be too. I couldn't forget that if things got dire.

I went cold.

What did Summer Shields being sensitive to magic mean for us? Part of me wanted to reach out and touch it—to feel it for myself. Maybe Trish was wrong. I could only hope she was wrong. Or that Summer would never figure out how to use said magic.

"What do you two want?" I made no pretense of being nice or obliging. That was for Agatha.

"Just a word," Summer said.

"With me? Cause Trish isn't here."

Jade examined her watch. "No, she won't be off for another two hours. I gave her the morning shift."

"That's why we came here now." Summer's sneer curled into a smirk. "What we have to say is for you, not her."

Jade nodded along. "We have a proposition for you."

"Whatever it is, I'm not interested."

"Listen—" Jade's attempt at sounding sincere was cringeworthy "—we're aware things between us, the three of us, haven't been great. We had a rocky start."

"And what happened at After Dark Con, we're sorry about that too."

"Truly, we are."

"And I don't blame you for what happened to my hair," Summer said. "That wasn't your spell, was it? That was Trish. Honestly, maybe I deserved it."

I tried not to give anything away. She was right. It was Trish's wards that had removed every hair on her head. Since then, she'd worn it in a pixie cut. Somehow it worked with the elongated shape of her face.

"I don't know what you want from me but—"

"It's something simple, really," Jade said.

Summer nodded this time. "We've come out as the hosts of *Creel Creek After Dark*. We show our faces now. We're kind of hoping you'll do the same. We want you to come out as a witch."

These chicks were crazier than I thought.

"Not on the show or anything. We'd just like to hear your side of the story. Tell us where we've gone wrong."

"And where we're right," Summer finished. "Cause we are right. At least about you... and a few others." Her eyes shot toward the door. But Agatha and her car were long gone.

"We saw everything at After Dark Con," Jade said.

"And in the graveyard before that."

"The graveyard that's just so conveniently disappeared since that show." Jade cocked her head. "Tell me that's a coincidence. Tell me I've lost my way in the woods I've explored since I was a little girl."

I didn't say a word. Anyway, I was already tired of lying to these two. Mostly, I was tired of their obsession with us. It was fine by me if they obsessed over the supernatural world. But why us? What had we ever done to them?

Okay, what had we done that wasn't provoked?

"Your face tells us everything we need to know," Jade said.

I blinked. Briefly, I wondered if I put my intent toward pushing them out the door if my magic would just work like it did with Agatha's book.

Jade said to Summer, "I told you this wasn't going to work."

"Wait," I said. I didn't know exactly why. "I thought you said something about a proposition."

"That's right, we did." Summer smiled wider. If she thought she had me in her trap, she was wrong. I was sure that was just the inner me wanting to get the full picture.

"You were at the vineyard the other morning," she continued. "That's how many crime scenes you've been privy to? Every single one since you found the bloodsucker?"

"Don't call him that," Jade scolded.

Summer just shrugged.

"Okay..."

Summer rolled her eyes. "Right. Our colleague, Jami

Castel, was found dead. And your Subaru was parked there that morning."

"I'm not hearing a proposal here, Summer."

"If you help us, we can help you. Not only can we help your boyfriend, we also know you'd be just as interested in Jami's work as we are."

"If it's something you didn't tell Dave, then that's a crime. Withholding evidence."

"We can't tell him what we don't know," Summer said. "That's the whole point. He has everything of Jami's—her laptop, her research. Her car. Everything."

"And what, you want me to steal it?"

"No! Of course not. You don't have to do anything illegal."

"The proposal is this," Jade said. "We can help get into her files—help find the videos she planned to release on ParaTube. After we do that, you can tell us about being a witch."

"It seems to me you just want access to those videos."

"Well, yeah, that's part of it."

"Dave has people working on this. I doubt he'll even let me see what he finds."

"He might," Summer said. "At least what she had pertaining to you and the people you call friends."

"But Jami didn't even know me..."

"Just like you don't know us. Not really."

"Our word is our bond," Summer said stubbornly. "Whoever Dave has working for him, they aren't as good as me. They won't be able to find this stuff. She's hidden the files away."

"How can you be sure?"

"She told us she was onto something big. Something major. Just trust me. Trust us."

"The whole point is I can't trust either of you."

"We get that. We do. Tell you what, final offer, whatever we find on the computer, it goes through you whether we're allowed to share it on ParaTube or not."

"I don't think—"

"Either trust us or don't." Frustrated, Jade flipped the blonde hair out of her face.

"Jade!"

"I told you this wasn't going to work. We can go about it another way."

"There is no other way," Summer said through clenched teeth. "Her laptop has everything."

"No. Everything lives in the cloud these days. Let's just backtrack Jami's last steps. She was at the library the day before the Harvest Festival."

"Okay."

"What about—"

"I have another idea." Jade smirked in my direction. "There are other ways to get her on our side."

Doubtful.

Summer rolled her eyes again, this time at Jade, then rounded on me. "Just think about it, okay? We'll come back next week. Until then, let's call a truce. We won't try to blow your cover, or your friends', and y'all don't cast any hexes on us."

My comeback left a lot to be desired. "Sure, whatever. I'll think about it."

The strange part was it wasn't a lie. They'd actually given me a lot to think about.

15

IN WITCH WE GO SHOPPING

I had kept the encounter with Jade and Summer secret, at least for now, not telling Trish or Gran—Dave either. And Brad hadn't come back from the shadow realm.

I couldn't pinpoint exactly why I was keeping it under wraps. It wasn't like I'd ever stoop to their level.

Would I?

Absolutely, not, I told myself. *You're better than that—better than them!*

But still, I couldn't muster the nerve to talk with Dave about it.

He fiddled with the radio in the minivan, found a Christmas station, and left it there. He absentmindedly checked the rearview mirror. The backseats were empty. "I feel terrible, sticking Imogene with them another day. But I've got to get this shopping done or I never will."

"Or," I singsonged, "you could've shopped from your laptop at work. Online shopping—it's fast and easy. And you don't have to look anyone in the face."

"I happen to like looking people in the face." He turned his head, and it gave me an antsy, uncomfortable feeling.

"Look at the road."

A sign informed us we were nearing Charlottesville. I did my own check of the mirrors. My usual shadow wasn't there. I hadn't seen the owl since the confrontation with Jade and Summer.

Dave huffed. "I don't really trust online shopping. I've seen so much identity theft, so much fraud—like *so* much fraud—that I think I'll keep my credit card in my pocket, thanks."

"How much fraud have you seen?"

"Enough. Trust me. Plugging your credit card in online is a slippery slope."

I frowned. "I think most sites are reasonably secure. At least, the big ones are."

"Yeah, but I don't like shopping at the big stores. I want my money to go to a child's college fund, not a hedge fund."

"So, where are we going, then? I thought you said the mall?"

"There are mom and pop shops at the mall, Constance. In fact, these days, it's almost fifty-fifty. Malls are on the way out. But this place, ah," he sighed exaggeratedly, "I hope they never shut their doors."

"Okay..." I arched an eyebrow.

But he didn't elaborate. I had to wait. He was right about malls. Even at the start of Christmas shopping season, the parking was plentiful and the crowds just middling. There were still several household names amongst the stores, but at least two or three retail storefronts were vacant, shuttered with their metal gates down.

And no one even tried to spritz perfume on my wrist, or sell me anything for that matter, from a kiosk. There was a father and son team at a small cart outside the food court with a booming business. The father was selling while the son put on a demonstration, flying one of the many drones they had for sale. It soared high above our heads and came in for a landing next to a fountain. My heart lurched as he neared it—I was afraid it would fall in the water. But he maneuvered it expertly away.

The food court smelled like a typical food court—the mingling of various fried foods and the sweet scent of Cinnabon wafted through the air. We got a quick bite to eat then headed off to our destination.

Dave was holding my hand and it surprised me when we came to a jerky stop. "This is it. What do you think?"

We had stopped outside a storefront. Its dinky sign read Bill's Frisbees & More. There were a few old-fashioned toys in the display window—Lincoln Logs, metal cars, and a frisbee or two—alongside some newer Lego sets.

Inside, it was much the same, a mid-size store, not quite as small as the candle shop but nowhere near as big as the department stores at the end of each corridor. The store was split in two, between nostalgic toys from our youth and probably Gran's as well on the right and the newer toys with their hefty prices on the left. Dave *would* be contributing to someone's fund and depleting his own. That was for sure.

"Isn't it great?" He sniffed the air. It smelled stale, almost like Bewitched Books.

"It's something," I agreed. "You're sure you can find the girls' gifts here?"

"Maybe not all their gifts." He shrugged. "But I have to find something. It's tradition. They always get something from here. And they always will, if I can help it."

"Always?"

He smiled. "It's something Becky and I started. When we

were kids, this place had the best commercials—especially around Christmas time. They'd come on between Saturday morning cartoons. I used to beg my mom to take me here."

"Did she?"

"Never." He laughed. "But that's the beauty of being an adult. I get to make my own traditions. Becky and I started this one for Allie's first Christmas. That baby doll is around somewhere, even if she doesn't play with it as much as she used to."

The toy shop wasn't exactly Duncan's Toy Chest—a.k.a. FAO Schwarz—from *Home Alone 2*. But then again, I could see how as a kid, Dave had probably held it in that sort of regard.

"What other traditions do you have?"

"Let's see. We do Christmas Eve the same every year. We bake cookies—Becky's recipe." He put the back of his hand to his mouth and whispered, "I think it's really Betty Crocker's."

I smiled.

"After we set out the cookies, the girls watch a movie, and they get to open a present—they get to pick from under the tree. Then it's bed."

"That sounds nice," I said. "My dad and I had traditions like that. But we kind of let them go once I was old enough—if you know what I mean. We watched a movie on Christmas Eve though. Every year."

"What movie?"

"Well, he was particular to *Scrooged*. My preference is always *White Christmas*."

"You and my mother would've gotten along."

"I'm guessing yours is *Die Hard*?"

"Nice try," he laughed. "But I, too, am a stickler for the classics. Give me *Ernest Saves Christmas* any day. Just kidding. It's *A Christmas Story* for me. You think Kacie is ready for a BB gun?"

"No!"

He grinned. We walked up and down the aisles in search of the perfect gift for each girl. There were some contenders but nothing really stood out. He found something for Kacie—being the youngest, she was easier to pick for than the other two. Finally, he found a gift for Allie. That left Elsie.

At the back of the store, the wall was covered in frisbees, most of which were for playing disc golf. I doubted it started that way. Dave picked one up and tossed it a few feet in the air. "What do you think? Everyone loves frisbees, right?"

"Not eight-year-old girls," I said.

"No," Dave sighed. "Eight-year-old girls want cats."

"That they do." I hadn't forgotten about Licorice or the deal the girls had made with me. It just never seemed like the right time for our big reveal. I was keeping too many secrets.

But it wasn't the right time to tell him. I had to warn them first. I changed the subject fast.

"What other traditions did you have as a kid? Anything else you're holding on to?"

"A few," he said. "My mom's Christmas French toast. And I typically make a batch of her fruitcakes by now, but I've been distracted."

"Fruitcake?" I wasn't partial to it and it showed on my face.

"I'm not a big fan either. And the girls won't even try it."

"Who eats it?"

"I take a few to the office, a couple to city hall, some other places." He drew me closer, wrapping his arm around me. "Again, it's about the tradition. You down for helping a guy out in the kitchen this evening? There *will* be other helpers present. And the main job is to help clean up after them."

"I think I can do that." I smiled.

It took ages, but Dave finally settled on a present for Elsie. He was far less particular at Target on the way out of town, picking up multiple gifts. The back rows of the van were full to the brim. I only hoped he wasn't planning on hiding anything in the garage.

Turns out, he wasn't.

"Oh, no, definitely not there," he said. "They'd find them in a heartbeat. I swear, they're out there all the time right now. It's their favorite place to play."

Really? You don't say…

"Are you okay?" he asked. "Is something on your mind?"

"There's a lot," I told him, which was true enough. Shopping had brought back a flood of memories, not all of them good—like my first Christmas without my mother. And this would be my first without my father.

Even the good memories made me want to cry. Then there was everything else, the recent murder, everything with the Faction, and the owl not automagically turning into my mother like I'd hoped it would. I checked behind us again. She wasn't there.

He nodded and stared out at the road. "I know what this is about."

"You do?"

He nodded again. "It's Becky, isn't it? It makes you uncomfortable when I talk about her."

"Uh… no. Definitely not. I understand you had a life before me. I had one too. Remember? I was married."

"Yeah. But it—"

"It ended badly?" I studied his face. He was in full 'oh crap, I said the wrong thing' mode.

"Yeah, it ended badly," I said, not as delicately as I meant it. "But believe it or not, I was happy for some of it. Most of it, really. Just the ending made it sour."

Endings do that...

"I didn't mean to—"

"You didn't offend me," I said. "It's all right."

I decided to let him off without even a warning. Sometimes, I do that for the people I care about the most.

"This might sound weird," Dave said. "But I think my story is the opposite of yours. The way it ended makes me look back on everything through rose-tinted glasses. I kind of hope they never break."

"They won't. And you can talk about Becky as much as you want to. I completely understand. She factors into your life in a big way. She always will."

"I'm glad you see it that way. That's how I see it. But it's hard, you know? I wasn't sure you'd understand."

"I do."

He squinted, his eyes on the horizon, and his lips curved into a smile. "Hey, I thought you were married twice."

I glowered at him. "You're lucky I like you, Dave Marsters."

We were almost back to Creel Creek when I decided to broach the subject of the computer. My conversation with the podcasters had been weighing on me. I wasn't going to do things their way, not without trying every other avenue first.

"Hey, you haven't said anything about Jami's murder all day."

"I was going for a record," he said. "And there's not much to tell. I thought we decided you were staying out of it?"

"No. We said I wouldn't do any sleuthing. And I haven't."

Granted, I hadn't had much opportunity.

"What do you wanna know?" His voice tightened.

"I was thinking about online shopping again and Jami's computer came to mind."

"Oh," he said, softening a little. "Nothing on there. Nothing pertinent at least. We cracked it open and went through every file."

"You didn't find any videos? Nothing she'd been putting together for her channel or to blackmail someone else?"

He shook his head. "Nothing like that."

"Oh…" In a way, it was a relief. I'd been afraid she had something on me or Trish. Or worse, Gran. There was only a slight prickling at the back of my brain, telling me that the files were hidden and that Summer could find them. But I pushed those thoughts aside.

"And the folders?" I asked.

"Not much there, either. Well, nothing aside from the photos she was using to blackmail Cyrus. She made copies and had them in two separate folders—in case she lost them, I guess. Funny though…"

"Funny why?"

"Two reasons. Funny because there were four photos, only three of which had Cyrus or Caulfield in them."

"The fourth?"

"No one recognizable, not to me or to anyone we've asked."

"I could take a look. Gran could."

"That might be helpful actually," he said, and it didn't sound begrudging.

His hand grazed my knee. I took it and squeezed, lost in the thought of what that picture might hold. It occurred to me that he hadn't finished what he was going to say. "What's the other reason?"

"Oh, yeah, that. The photos are just copies. Copies of

copies. The originals are at the library. I asked Cyrus if he wanted us to have them destroyed, but he said no."

"Do you think he'll do it himself?"

"I don't think he cared. He's preoccupied with other things."

"The disappearance of Mr. Caulfield."

"Exactly that." Dave squeezed my hand, more gently than I had his. "I'm guessing this means you haven't had any epiphanies..."

"None."

"Me either. Now it's a waiting game to see if forensics or maybe the computer lead us somewhere else."

"What about the boyfriend and his wife?"

"We brought them in a couple times. I don't see either as a suspect. In the meantime, I've been talking with her family and former employers."

"Her family?"

"They were estranged. She's been living out of her car for about a year."

"And employers? I thought she did freelance."

"She did a lot of things. A jack of all trades—as long as the trade was something literary. She was a ghostwriter, a personal assistant, and yes, a freelancer. She did some editing and writing for various things. We were able to find records of payments through her PayPal account, but that's about it."

"Any leads there?"

He shook his head and pursed his lips. "None. Aside from her family, everyone seemed to love her. Everyone except Cyrus..."

16

IN WITCH THE SLEUTHING STARTS

It was Wednesday, Trish's day off at the grocery store. She didn't really need me at the bookstore, but I was there anyway. There wasn't much else to do this first week of December with Dave at work, his girls at school, and Gran being Gran.

She still refused to tell me what the kerfuffle at the graveyard was all about. She was already asking about the upcoming winter solstice, wondering if I had plans. I didn't. I wasn't planning to attend, and I doubted many of the other witches would show, either.

Even Agatha was steering clear of our house on her daily walks. No doubt, she was perturbed at Gran for not sharing the secret.

I guess we all have our secrets, some bigger than others.

Trish huffed as I fiddled with the espresso machine. I frothed milk and poured it over an espresso shot, trying my hand at latte art. It was more like latte finger paint, maybe a flower or perhaps a giraffe.

"That sucks," I muttered. "I thought I had this one."

"More importantly, how does it taste?" Trish yawned,

looking a lot more interested in the coffee drink than she had last time.

I sipped. "Hmm. Not bad. Good, actually."

"That's nice." She smiled and flicked her purple streak out of her face. "You think I'm kidding. But I swear, it's only a matter of time. Jade's going to fire me. The way she looks at me these days."

I squirmed uncomfortably behind the machine. The need—or rather, the want—to tell Trish about Jade and Summer's proposition bubbled in my throat. But I knew Trish's opinions on the matter without needing her to speak them, so I held my tongue.

It doesn't matter, I thought. They hadn't come back. And anyway, I didn't have the computer.

"It's going to be fine," I told Trish, and something in me agreed it was true. "For what it's worth, I do believe you. Jade is Jade."

"She is. I'm counting on you." Trish inched closer. "Hey, make me something with chocolate. I need a boost."

I set to work on a peppermint mocha.

Tis the season.

Trish grabbed the coffee as soon as I was done. She tasted. "Yeah, that's nice. I think maybe we should advertise."

"Really? What's our advertising budget?"

She laughed. "I'll have to get back to you on that."

I practiced making shots—wasting milk was expensive. Trish went to the back room, returned, and set her coffee down on the counter. Her eyes narrowed suspiciously. They darted up and down the shelves, then she felt around behind the register, moving books and papers like she'd lost something. "Uh, where's Twinkie?"

"Helping Brad in the shadow realm."

"Still?"

I nodded.

"Shouldn't there be like a statute of limitations on these things? They've tried hard enough, but it's looking like Mr. Caulfield's not coming back."

I stiffened. "Trish, there's no statute of limitations on murder, so..."

"I know—I know there isn't. I was just saying. Sorry. I didn't mean to offend."

"It's okay."

"I'm guessing there's been no traction there either. The murder, I mean."

"Not much."

At Thanksgiving, I'd told Trish what I knew about Jami's murder, which wasn't very much. We went over the new details, the little there were.

"I'm a little surprised you haven't started your own investigation." Trish smirked. "Or have you?"

I shook my head. "You sound like Dave."

"How so?"

"He makes it out like I'm on the lookout for trouble."

"Well, you did go around asking about the Faction for months."

"And the Faction didn't end up being the bad guys..."

"Good point." Trish shrugged. "And back to my point... I didn't actually mean it negatively. It was more a question. Hey, are you investigating?"

"I said I'm not." I probably sounded as exasperated as I felt.

"Yeah. But why not?" She looked skeptical.

"Because! Wait. Why are you so interested?"

She cocked her head in playful contemplation, as if the question were much more thought provoking than it was. "If

I'm being honest—which I *always* am—playing murder mystery with you is kind of fun."

The sincere honesty sent another pang of guilt through me. "Dave doesn't want me to."

"And we *always* do what Dave wants?"

"Don't remind me." Another, bigger, pang of guilt. That was a low blow—another secret, a secret Trish knew about, if slightly more innocent.

"What? What am I not reminding you of, again?"

"The cat," I said. I'd told her about that, almost right after it happened. I had to tell someone.

"Oh? You haven't told him about that yet? I thought you were going to tell him. Why haven't you? He hasn't found it?"

"No. And I've got to warn the girls. I was kind of hoping the magic would wear off and then it wouldn't look as much like my fault when he—"

"Rehomes it?" she guessed.

"I hope not. I meant when he finds it."

"So, that means your magic *hasn't* worn off."

"No."

"Magic plays by its own rules. As should you."

"What does that mean?"

She glowered at me. "You know what it means! I want to know more about Jami Castel—why she was murdered. What's next in the investigation?"

I shrugged.

Trish rolled her eyes. "I'm disappointed in you. Really, you can't think of anywhere we could go to get a tidbit of detail? I'm not talking suspects here. You don't have to go against Dave's wishes. But there has to be something we could do—somewhere to go. Leave no stone unturned and all that."

That phrase struck me as odd for some reason, but I couldn't put my finger on why. Then it occurred to me why —there were stones or rocks in Jami's car. Not to mention the folders with the photos in them.

And hadn't Jade mentioned something about retracing Jami's steps?

"I guess we could try the library."

"The library?" Trish raised a painted-on eyebrow. "I was hoping for somewhere fun, not depressing."

"It's where she found those pictures of Cyrus..."

"You've seen them?"

I shook my head. "Dave has them."

Trish rolled her eyes again and swept her keys from the counter beside the register. "Fine... we'll go to the library."

∽

WE GOT into Trish's canary yellow Volkswagen Beetle and she drummed her fingers on the wheel, waiting for me to buckle up. Beside her, the small vase—standard in all new Beetles—held an artificial black orchid—not so standard.

She fired up the car, and a plume of black smoke billowed from the back.

It was a short drive to the library, down the access road by the park. The Creel Creek Library was hidden behind it —and not only by the trees. The red brick facade was covered in ivy. Unmaintained, it grew up the walls and over some windows. There were at least two stories and a basement level that protruded from the ground slightly like a bi-level home.

The parking lot was small as if they never expected a crowd. While the building could hold hundreds, the lot was a row of ten parking spots in front of the massive black doors.

Trish eased into a parking space beside a Ford Thunderbird—the retro remake, not the classic.

"Wow. I haven't been here since I was a little girl." Trish craned her neck over the steering wheel.

"So, it's changed?" I thought at least the ivy was new. Or it had grown over thirty years since Trish was a girl.

"No," she scoffed. "That's why I said wow. It looks exactly the same."

"Really?"

"I already told you, I *always* tell the truth."

"Saying it like that makes it sound like I don't."

She shrugged a shoulder. "If the shoe fits... you know I can tell when you're keeping something from me, right?" I went to argue but she put out a hand. "Just tell me when you're ready. I don't need an excuse or a lie."

That certainly put me in my place. I wondered if Trish had gotten two gifts—her magical sensitivity thing and the ability to sniff out the truth. Maybe Mother Gaia had given me none. It would explain a lot.

Trish had probably developed this power of observation on her own, through years and years of study.

Or I'm just a terrible liar.

We walked up the steps and I heaved open the door. While I'd run past the library on occasion and gone to the park with Dave and his girls, I'd never set foot inside until now.

Trish had thought the exterior was unchanged. The inside was evidently also unchanged, boasting no modern amenities like, well, most libraries. There were just a couple of computers. And it still maintained a massive card catalog right next to the information desk.

Otherwise, it was a library. The books were spread out and divided into sections. There was a whole room devoted to periodicals. There were quiet rooms, a children's area, and tables with those uncomfortable wooden chairs scattered throughout the main room.

It smelled like a library, more stale than Bewitched Books and even more dusty. And like Bewitched Books, it was empty, save a single librarian.

"It's Mrs. Hayes," Trish whispered.

The acoustics were amazing. Her voice carried across the room. The little old woman wheeled around, looking confused.

"Sorry, Mrs. Hayes." Trish waved and half smiled. She almost looked intimidated by the little old woman.

"Did you need something?" Mrs. Hayes adjusted her glasses. Her buggy eyes bulged at Trish with her black eyeliner, purple lipstick, and purple streak of hair to match.

"Maybe," Trish said.

"It's a yes or no question. And please, do keep your voice down."

Trish's green eyes swept the room. There was no one there but us. And the stereotypical librarian of doom.

The woman had to be pushing a hundred. That and she was pushing a hundred pounds of books on a library cart. Or she was trying to. It hadn't moved yet.

"We're looking for the photo archives," I said, probably too loud. She flinched. "Sorry, we're looking for the photo archives," I whispered.

"Is there, like, an online catalog?" Trish asked.

Mrs. Hayes pursed her lips in what could've been a frown. "The photos are in the basement. No catalog. We had an intern who was supposed to do something with that."

"When was that?"

"1998," Mrs. Hayes said.

"Oh... well, we'll just look around and get out of your hair."

The old woman nodded and bent down against the cart, shouldering it to get it moving. It creaked forward.

There was a spiral staircase leading downstairs. I was expecting stacks. But the basement was a dimly lit, dank, and divided into rooms with sturdy closed doors. We found the door labeled Photo Archive and went in.

"Remember how I told you it's normally fun to play murder mystery with you?"

"Yeah?"

"I take it back. This place gives me the creeps. I'm getting some serious *Ghostbusters* vibes down here. And this looks like work."

She was right. There were dozens of filing cabinets, where I assumed photos were stored. There were also bookshelves with what looked to be old family photo albums. Upon closer inspection, that's exactly what they were.

"So, Jami found those photos in here?" Trish asked.

"I think so."

"You know, I kind of wondered why no one else had until now."

"Same," I said.

There was some hope. The filing cabinets were labeled by decade, from the late 1800s to as recent as 1998, probably when that intern was working down here.

I opened a filing cabinet—1960s—and peeked inside, hoping for folders and a filing system. I was severely disappointed. There were photos of all sizes stacked on top of each other, close to spilling out. Some Polaroids had been rubber-banded together, but they were the exception, not the norm.

"This would be tough, wouldn't it? I mean, if there were no such thing as magic."

Trish, the master of summoning spells, muttered a few words under her breath. She reached out, her hand caressing the air, and a few cabinets began to shake.

That was when the door opened.

17

IN WITCH WE GET LIBRARY CARDS

The filing cabinet stopped shaking, and the room went eerily quiet. In this room like this, in the drab basement of an almost deserted library, the lack of sound was even more eerie. It felt like air had been taken as well, like the door was an airlock to outer space.

Trish's outstretched arm dropped, and her eyes went wide. Mrs. Hayes stood in the doorway with her glasses off. She was wiping them down with a tissue, not paying attention to the room. It was hard to tell if she'd seen anything or even if she'd heard it.

She looked up, nonchalant as she adjusted the spectacles on her nose. "You girls finding what you need?"

"I think so." Trish scurried to a filing cabinet and yanked it open.

"I'm not busy anymore," Mrs. Hayes said. "So, I'm free to help. I helped that girl who came down here last. The girl who died. Did y'all hear about that?"

"We did," I answered. "It's sad."

"It is," Trish agreed. Then she asked Mrs. Hayes the

obvious question, "By any chance, do you remember what she was down here looking for?"

Mrs. Hayes considered the question. "This and that, mostly. A little of everything. She never told me what she was doing with the things she found. I thought maybe she was working on one of those—oh, documentaries!"

"Maybe she was," I said.

"What kind of help did you give her?" Trish asked.

"Well, my eyesight isn't what it used to be. I didn't help her down here so much. She had other help. Mostly, I held on to some pictures for her as she came and went."

"How many did she collect?" Trish shut the drawer.

"Dozens and dozens, maybe a hundred or so altogether. Some, she had to make copies of at the Walmart. That kind of machine is expensive, so we don't have one here."

"Is there a special place she put them when she was done?"

Mrs. Hayes pursed her lips. "Well, there's a stack on my desk upstairs. I couldn't bring myself to put them back. I guess I was hoping she might come around again."

Trish and I locked eyes. We could take a look at them. It was probably better than sifting through whatever was down here.

We followed Mrs. Hayes up the stairs. She took them one at a time and rested heavily on the rail between steps. "May I ask what got you girls interested in all this?"

"Oh, well, it's kind of a long story. Jami stopped by our bookstore."

"That doesn't sound like a very long story." Her brow furrowed in concentration. "You mean that store with those magical books—the store on Main Street?"

"It was my mother's store," Trish blurted out, as if to prevent Mrs. Hayes from saying something she might regret.

Not that she seemed the type to regret her words... ever. She reminded me of Gran in that regard.

The older woman shrugged and took the next step. "We have some like those on the second floor. You should check them out if you get a chance."

"I'll do that," Trish said.

Mrs. Hayes didn't turn around, but she cocked her head in a way that said she didn't believe Trish. "Go on, tell me more about Jami. The news hasn't said a thing about it. And the police never stopped by. Not even after I called and told them she was here many times the last month or two."

"That often?"

"Alone, most of the time. Two times, there was a man with her. Another time, a woman."

"Did you recognize them?"

"I didn't. We don't get many visitors." Mrs. Hayes shook her head. And we finally made it to the top step. "Then again, I wouldn't have recognized you, Trisha Harris, had you not mentioned your mother."

"Trisha?" I smirked. Trish's eyes shot daggers at me.

Mrs. Hayes was faster on level ground. We got to her desk and she rummaged through it, finding a stack of old photos about an inch thick. She handed them across and Trish took them.

"Can we take them home with us?"

"If you bring them back."

"We will... I will."

"Like you'll look over our magic books?"

"I will!" Trish's voice went higher.

"Then you'll need a library card. I know for a fact yours is no longer valid."

"Next time," Trish said curtly. "This is more than enough to hold us for today."

"I'm sure it is." Mrs. Hayes looked displeased, and Trish was already halfway out of her chair.

"What did Jami do?" The question seemed to come out of nowhere, but it definitely came from Mrs. Hayes's mouth.

I took it upon myself to answer. "Oh, she did a lot of things. She was a writer, an editor, a ghostwriter."

"A ghostwriter, you say. Kind of like Hope Evans?"

"Hope who?"

"Oh, well, I guess you wouldn't know her, would you? And I doubt her books are your cup of tea—you two seem more the fantasy sort. No offense."

She definitely meant to be offensive.

"What does Hope write?" Trish asked.

"Oh, you know that guy on TV—with those books on unsolved mysteries?"

Trish looked at me. I shrugged. There weren't quite a million of those authors, but the list was long enough.

"I, uh... no."

"You know," she prattled on, "the guy who specializes in mysteries with a supernatural flair. He's always on the History channel but offers little substance on the matter. He speculates on ancient aliens and paranormal coverups. Bill something or other."

"Bill..." Trish concentrated, "... Bill Abraham?"

"That's him!"

I nodded encouragingly. It wasn't that long ago he had a book out and had done the rounds on morning TV, ahead of *The Price Is Right*—Gran's favorite show.

"Never wrote a book in his life," Mrs. Hayes said. "He does the TV specials and the tours, but it's Hope who puts the words on the page. Used to be, she came by the library to do her research. But these days, she has *other* ways of getting the information she needs."

"Wait... she lives here in town?"

"That's what I was trying to tell you, wasn't it?" Mrs. Hayes scowled. "Maybe Jami—if she was a ghostwriter as you say—maybe she knew Hope."

"Maybe so." I smiled at Trish.

"She interviewed me once for a book about the mine disaster. My great-great-grandaddy died in the explosion."

"That's interesting. I wasn't aware there was a book about the mine." Aside from the graveyard, there was no evidence a mine ever existed at all.

"It covers several topics," she said. "All about unexplained disasters—in fact, I think that's the name of the book. Hope could tell you more about it."

"She could," Trish agreed, "if we knew where to find her."

I leveled my smile from Trish to Mrs. Hayes. "Do you happen to have Miss Evans' address?"

"This is a library, not the phone book." She sighed. "I guess they don't make those anymore, either."

"No worries," I said. "We understand."

Mrs. Hayes frowned again, like this wasn't the outcome she'd wanted. In fact, the whole time we'd been there it seemed like she wanted to draw out our conversation. She was as interested in Jami Castel as we were, for what seemed to be the same reasons. Or similar.

"Tell you what," she said. "I'll make you girls library cards. And maybe, just maybe, while I'm doing that, I'll accidentally leave the file open to Hope's address."

Trish stifled a chuckle. "I think we'll be fine without library cards, Mrs. Hayes. Constance here is dating the sheriff. Getting the address won't be a problem."

Mrs. Hayes wasn't laughing. She reached her hand out and covered the photos across the desk. "You know, I've changed my mind. You may check those photographs out with a library card. That's the deal."

"Fine," Trish said.

"And you, dear? Would you like a card?"

What Trish had said wasn't exactly true. I couldn't ask Dave for the address without him knowing I was doing a little sleuthing.

"It'll only take a minute," Mrs. Hayes continued. "Assuming you have your driver's licenses handy. And I can loan you a copy of that Dan Abraham book—*Unexplained Disasters*."

"You know, that sounds good." I fished in my purse for my wallet. "I think I would like one."

"That's the spirit, dear." For the first time since we'd met her, Mrs. Hayes smiled.

18

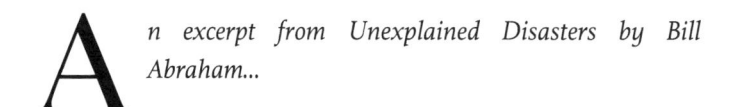

UNEXPLAINED DISASTERS

An excerpt from Unexplained Disasters by Bill Abraham...

ABOUT THE AUTHOR

William "Bill" Abraham was born in Biloxi, Mississippi. His father was in the Air Force and his mother was a nurse. He lived the typical military brat life, moving from place to place throughout his youth, and he believes the term brat is apropos when referring to everything about his childhood. He graduated with a B.A. in Communications from Louisiana State University in 1986.

After graduation, Bill moved to Los Angeles to pursue acting. His acting career was short-lived. After only securing small roles in both TV and film, Bill became a researcher on the show *Ancient Mysteries* where he was featured in several episodes. Bill went on to host *Supernatural Skies*, *Paranormal Murders*, and *Occult Atrocities*, as well as consulting for many other shows on The History Channel.

Bill's books have all been New York Times bestsellers. *Salem Sorcery: The Lead Up to the Witch Trials* spent nearly a year on the Hardcover Nonfiction list.

When he's not making TV shows or writing, Bill can be found in California with his wife, Maria, and their three schnauzers.

PREFACE

This book isn't quite like my others. You'll notice, for one, it's a great deal thicker. Also, it covers many topics—many disasters—while my other books, to this point, have focused on a single topic.

There are many reasons for this. The research started, as it almost always does, with newspaper clippings. I came across several of these smaller stories while researching my other books. I set each clipping aside, intending to go back to them later, when time allowed. All of them felt like they might be whole books on their own.

But time never allowed. While I tried, I never could make a strong enough case to the publisher that any of these stories deserved their own book. Finally, I convinced my editor to allow me to combine them into a book. That book is what you see before you.

As always, when gathering facts and testimony for this book, I was but a ghost in the room—an observer jotting down notes and asking the odd question or two. In no way did I influence or steer the stories in any direction.

Any speculation about the supernatural comes from the people involved, from firsthand accounts and oral histories. I encourage you, as I do, to keep an open mind.

Bill Abraham
Los Angeles, 2018

THE CREEL CREEK COAL MINE COLLAPSE OF 1830 AND THE COVERUP THAT FOLLOWED

Settled in the late 1700s and located in the foothills of the Blue Ridge Mountains, Creel Creek, Virginia was named for its founder, Herman Creel. The town grew as Creel's family grew, with eight boys, who each had many boys of their own. To this day, almost fifteen percent of the population of Creel Creek bares the last name Creel.

The Creels built a small inn that served as both post office and tavern. It also served as a stopover for anyone who wandered through on their way to the University of Virginia from the western half of the state, later to be West Virginia.

But aside from the Creels, the town's growth was small. In 1830, Creel Creek was little more than a mining town, with neighbors Lynchburg and Charlottesville seeing much steadier increases in population.

The Creel Creek Coal Company was founded in 1828 by Samuel Jonathan Smith, his brother David, and three other individuals covered in later chapters.

Together, they secured ownership of mining rights in the

foothills and hired locally at first. Later, they took out an advertisement in the *Virginia Advocate*, claiming wages of up to $1.50 a day.

Few records from the era remain. But I was able to create a picture of the Creel Creek Coal Company by using the town's wealth of archived data, along with newspaper clippings, mortuary records, and state mining records.

The final piece of the puzzle came when I unearthed a few annual business reports in the University of Virginia library and linked those to the Creel family.

While the Creels had taken no part in mining coal, surely believing it to be beneath them, they didn't mind sharing in the profits. Melvin Creel, Herman's grandson, had a ten percent stake in the Creel Creek Coal Company. It's from his journals and the accounts of his descendants that I gleaned much of the information presented in this book.

We might assume the mine operated like any other coal mine, that they dug and constructed shafts. But actually, very little is known about the two-year period from the company's founding to the explosion that occurred in 1830.

Men went off to the mines and worked. They came home at night covered in dirt and grime. And they left early the next morning to do the same, over and over again.

In that time, Melvin Creel's stock increased in value. When the company closed shortly after the explosion in 1830, Melvin and his family moved to an estate outside of town worth the equivalent of two million dollars today.

Forgive me, I'm getting ahead of myself.

Two years had passed since the company's founding. One spring day in 1830 changed everything. An explosion rocked the area. According to Rowena Hayes—whose great-great-grandfather was in the mine at the time and whose great-great-grandmother was at home with her great-grandfather—the explosion shattered all of the windows in the row houses where the workers lived.

The remains of some thirty miners can be found in a small graveyard outside the Creel Creek city limits. Nearly twice that number died in the blast.

The news of the disaster didn't travel fast. It was only briefly mentioned in the *Virginia Advocate* and not until six months later.

Imagine that—an explosion that killed over sixty men was little more than a blip. I had to ask myself why that would be. At first, I thought it was a failure to research—a failure on my part. But after weeks and weeks of digging, so to speak, I concluded that the failure wasn't on my end.

No, it came down to something else entirely—a cover-up, both figurative and literal.

19

IN WITCH WE MEET A GHOST

Trish wasn't all that interested in speaking to the ghostwriter. Her fire for sleuthing had blown out.

From the library, we split up. I took home the book, and she took the stack of photos. But the next day, neither of us had made much headway. I'd skimmed a few pages of the book, finding the writing dry and the speculation lacking.

Trish had managed to find the three photos of Cyrus, but there was no telling what that elusive fourth photo contained, not without asking Dave for it.

I thought I would ease into it, asking again about Jami's laptop—if they'd gleaned any more information or found those videos. I knew they weren't a high priority for him.

"No luck," he said. "Are you really worried she was going to expose us?"

"It's a worry." I got brave. "Would you mind if maybe I took a peek at it?"

He softened. "I doubt it could hurt. I mean, as long as your magic's not going to erase anything like that Dresden guy's does."

"It shouldn't." I forced a laugh. It wasn't quite that bad, but it was true that magic and technology weren't exactly peas in a pod. I could only enchant things made of natural resources like wood and stone.

So, that was the computer taken care of. It didn't mean I was going to show it to Summer. At least, not definitively. But I could take a look and decide for myself if it was worth pursuing.

I asked about the pictures next—he'd already said I could see them. He told me he'd bring them home with the computer after his shift the next day.

With all the yeses in the air, it didn't seem like the right time to talk about the cat currently prowling his garage. So, I didn't, letting the girls off again.

I was troubled by the spell's effectiveness. The only reason I didn't lift it was because if Dave found her now, I'd be in trouble too.

Dave wasn't the only person to say yes that night. I relented and spent the night with him.

Trish and I reconvened at the store the next day. She grudgingly agreed to go with me to meet Hope Evans, despite thinking it was probably another dead end—just par for the course in the Jami Castel murder investigation.

"What can you tell me about the mine explosion?" I asked her on the way.

She shrugged. "Not much. It's not exactly covered in social studies."

"But you're aware it happened."

"Yeah... I mean, there's that plaque on the graveyard fence. And my mom talked about it a time or two. It's rumors and stuff."

"What kind of rumors?"

"They were mining magic, not coal." She succeeded in sounding both mystical and sarcastic.

"You don't buy that?"

"Well, I understand there's no evidence the company ever sold a lump of coal."

"Yeah. It said that in the book too. But it also said that the records were probably lost."

"Exactly. We can't just jump to magical conclusions... ya know, except when we can. It *is* Creel Creek."

"What about the other stuff?"

"You'll have to be more specific. What other stuff?"

"You know," I said, "the fact that the mine is nowhere to be found."

Trish shrugged again. "It got buried in the explosion."

"Yeah. The book said that too."

"See! That's why I gave you the book. I already knew that crap."

∽

HOPE EVANS LIVED in a gated subdivision—and definitely the nicest neighborhood in town with mortgages closing in on seven figures. How anyone in Creel Creek could afford such homes baffled me.

It was the same subdivision Mr. Caulfield had lived in before he died. I could only hope that Brad and Twinkie would be back today with news. It troubled me that he was missing. And my owl was missing.

And Trish was probably right—their window of opportunity to find him in the shadow realm was closing.

"You're sure about this?" she asked. I'd pulled Prongs near the gate and was eyeing the road.

"Sure. Why not?"

"Chances are this lady didn't even know Jami Castel."

"So you've said."

Trish made a face and sank into the passenger seat. "I mean, it won't hurt to knock her off our suspect list."

Scanning the road, I scowled. "We don't have a suspect list."

"Sure we do," she responded. "Cyrus—"

"Didn't do it."

"Still, he's on there with the boyfriend."

"Has an alibi."

"Okay. But suspects are still on the list, even if they're crossed off. Don't forget the boyfriend's wife..."

"Who was in the dark about the affair."

"If that's true, then who was the woman Jami met with at the library? Remember? Mrs. Hayes says she met two people there. If we assume the man she met was the boyfriend, then the woman might've been the wife. Maybe Jami came clean and set this whole thing in motion."

"That sounds sort of tragic," I said. "And it's a lot of assumptions. What do they say about assuming?"

"They say it, huh," Trish scoffed. "I've always wondered who this they is—if you ask me, it's them who are the assholes."

I gunned the engine and tailgated a white Yukon through the gate. We found Hope's house on the next street over. All the houses were brick, and they had a colonial feel with porch columns and painted shutters.

They were too nice and too clean. Most were decorated for Christmas with lights strung on roofs and the occasional inflatable in the yard, everything from the Grinch and Snoopy to a scale replica of Cousin Eddie's RV from *National*

Lampoon's Christmas Vacation which took up nearly half of Hope's neighbor's yard.

"I doubt that has HOA approval."

Trish laughed. "Definitely not."

It was a short walk from the car to the front door. Too short. I wasn't ready for the knock when Trish put her knuckles to the door. I wasn't sure what to expect of Hope Evans. A writer. A ghostwriter.

Maybe I expected someone ancient like Mrs. Hayes, not the smiling woman who answered the door—who could be no older than sixty. She had dark hair with a few stray grays. She wore fashionable clear glasses; they might've been for blue light. It being the afternoon, I gave her the benefit of the doubt, believing her outfit to be workout clothes and not cleverly disguised pajamas. Either way, she looked comfortable.

"May I help you?"

"Are you Hope Evans?" Trish asked.

"I am. What's this about?"

Trish and I both faltered.

I was never quick on my feet—or with my mouth. I usually relied on Trish in situations like this. And she relied on magic. But for some reason, Trish didn't say anything. She gave me one of her trademark looks. Obviously, I was supposed to have come up with something to say.

And I would have, had I not wasted precious time in the car talking with her.

Hope was quicker on the uptake. "You know, this neighborhood doesn't allow soliciting. I'll have to report you."

"We aren't soliciting," Trish said.

"No? What are you doing here?"

"We came to ask you some questions," I told her. "About the mine. About your book."

"My book?" Hope looked skeptical.

I dug *Unexplained Disasters* out of my purse and held it up.

"Oh... Oh! Someone's finally put it together. Did you two listen to that dreadful podcast I was on?"

"Yes," I said, at the same time Trish said, "No."

"Well, which is it?"

"Mrs. Hayes ratted you out," Trish told her.

"That sounds like her. I'm guessing she told you I interviewed her for this as well. That's how the two ladies found me. Forgive me if I'm not too keen for another interview like that."

"It won't be," I said. "We promise."

"You'll also understand if I don't trust your promises. We don't know each other." She regarded us. "But you do seem sincere. And I was kind of in need of a distraction. I'm on a deadline."

"When's your deadline?"

"Oh, that thing blew past a few weeks ago. I blocked out the interweb when it happened. Gives me an excuse when the publisher tries to email me about it." She opened the door wider. "Here, come in."

We followed her. The entryway led to a living room with high ceilings. There were built-in bookshelves around a modest sized TV hanging on the wall. From there, we went into the dining room. It boasted a modern rustic chandelier with Edison bulbs. There was a china cabinet on the far wall. A trick of the orangish light made it seem like the bone china moved when we walked in the room.

The room was just off the kitchen, which looked suitable for a cooking competition.

"Is that an ice cream maker?" Trish whispered.

"I think so," I mouthed back.

Hope gestured toward seats and sat opposite us, giving us the view of the immaculate kitchen and putting our backs to the china cabinet.

"This has been one of those books, you know," she continued our conversation from the door. "Stubborn like my last dachshund, Fiona."

"Mr. Abraham doesn't mind you're late?" I asked.

"I doubt he knows. Mostly, I work with the publisher directly. They'll call when things get dire. They can count on me. I've never let them down."

"So, you don't actually work with Mr. Abraham directly?"

"He doesn't talk to you at all?" Trish asked.

"I'm sure he knows I exist, if that's what you mean. And I know a lot about him—his whole backstory. I have to add tidbits amongst the research. But no, I've never spoken to the man myself. For a while, I was on good terms with his PA."

"That's nice, I guess." Trish said. "This is random, but you don't happen to work with any other ghostwriters? Or know any in the area?"

"Are you suggesting I'd farm the work out to others?" Hope was affronted. "You don't get to where I am in this business without putting out quality, every time."

"That's not what she was suggesting, Miss Evans. Not at all. No, I think she was wondering because of the recent murder. That girl was a ghostwriter too."

"A murder?" Hope squinted. "Sorry, I'm not up on current events. Like I said, I've had the internet off. Unfortunately, I'm able to play solitaire on my computer without it. What is this about a murder? You said she was a ghostwriter?"

"She was." Trish nodded. "Are you familiar with any nearby?"

"I can't say that I am. But I'm sorry for the loss. That's awful."

"It was," I said, dejected. Trish was right, of course. We were wasting our time here.

"We've gone and gotten ourselves distracted, haven't we? I'm often guilty of that. What was it you wanted to ask about this book? About the mine?"

I tightened my grip on the cover hoping the book would spark a question. She'd already answered everything I needed to know, which was that she didn't know Jami Castle.

So, what's the point?

I racked my brain for anything from the pages I'd skimmed that stuck out.

"Aren't you from Creel Creek?" I asked. "The way it read, it sounded like you'd stumbled upon the story."

"Good catch! I told you, I have to make it sound like Bill's voice—like he does on those TV shows he's on. I tried to make it sound like he came across it doing research.

"Growing up here, of course, I've known about it my whole life. I mean there wasn't a kid around who hadn't ventured to that graveyard at least once. We all knew the ghost stories and the legends."

Trish nodded. "Same here. I've lived here all my life."

Hope smiled. "My babysitter used to take me out near there to play hide-and-seek. I was always finding little treasures, and she'd take them as if they were hers. Rocks, mostly, and arrowheads, things like that. I used to get so aggravated with her.

"But that was then—when the only thing to do was go outside and play. Nowadays, the kids have their Gameboys and TVs in their rooms. They never set foot outside, if they can help it. I can tell. You can tell these things. It's in the fingernails. Mine were always dirty."

"Mine too." Trish held out her fingernails as if she expected them to still be dirty.

I shrugged. "I was in my room reading."

Which was true. For years after I thought my mother died, I preferred worlds of imagination to the real thing. Of course I never believed magic existed. Or that I would one day wield its power.

"I did plenty of that too," Hope admitted. "You saw my living room. And to be honest, I should probably cut this interview short. I have my own book to finish—or rather, I have to finish Bill's. I have to send my notes to his PA, so Bill will be prepped and ready for the next press tour."

"Does that mean he doesn't even read the book?" Trish asked.

"No. It just means *I'm* not convinced he does. Jami would never say as much. But Jami was fabulous. She's gone now. This new guy, Michael, is the worst."

"Jami?"

"That was her name, I think—Jami Castel. She was lovely."

My heart beat faster.

"Did you ever meet Jami?" Trish asked, leaning forward.

"A time or two. Why do you ask? And why are you both looking at me like that?"

"Hope," I also leaned forward, "what happened to Jami after she left Mr. Abraham's employ?"

"She was going into a private venture, I think. I wished her the best."

"But you don't know what happened to her after that?"

"When was the last time you spoke to her?" Trish asked.

"Ladies..." Hope moved her head from side to side, taking us in. "I'll answer your questions if you answer mine. Why are you so concerned about Jami Castel?"

"Because," I answered, "she's the ghostwriter we were talking about... who was murdered."

20

IN WITCH THERE'S A KNOCK AT THE DOOR

All this new information didn't seem like new information to Dave. He knew about Jami's visits to the library. He knew about her work with Bill Abraham, and he wasn't considering Hope Evans a suspect.

But neither was I.

Trish wasn't so quick to dismiss the connection. She added the ghostwriter's name to her mental list of suspects —a list I thought was lacking the most vital component... the killer.

As promised, Dave brought home the computer and the folder of photos that Jami had tried to use to blackmail Cyrus.

I spent the night there. I didn't really have a chance to pore over the evidence, not until Dave and the girls were gone for the day.

I flipped through the photos first. It was the same three that Trish had found in her stack—the photos clearly showed Cyrus looking the same age he looked today but at various points in time.

"So *Twilight*," I said to myself.

The fourth picture, we would never have found. There was no Cyrus, no man in the image at all. There were just two girls—an older girl, probably sixteen or seventeen, holding a black cat, and a younger girl, around Allie or Elsie's age. They were smiling. The picture was in color but faded, making the girls' faces blurry and unrecognizable. They could be anyone. A faded scrawl in marker on the back read **1971**, and in pencil, someone else had jotted "*the mine?*" with a question mark.

Perhaps that was Jami's pencil. Was she interested in the mine? Did Hope Evans mean more to the investigation than Trish and I thought?

I put the folder away and concentrated on the laptop. Dave had warned me what I'd find. Namely, nothing. They'd figured out her password somehow. It was on a sticky note stuck to the lid.

She was smart. She hadn't used a simple phrase. It was gobbledygook, random letters and numbers that made a pattern on the keyboard.

I typed it in. Her desktop background greeted me.

I searched through every folder and came to the same conclusion Dave had—that whatever she was making for ParaTube didn't live on this device. Or it was hidden in a way I'd never find it.

I packed up, taking the laptop and the folder with me, and went to Gran's house. I found it as quiet and uninhabited as Dave's had been, or almost. Brad was asleep inside a mountain of blankets and afghans on the couch. Only his nose and an eye were visible.

"Gran? Stevie?"

"They've flown the coop," Brad boomed. "Took off in the car about an hour ago."

I had to poke my head into the garage to see it with my own eyes. The Buick was gone. "Where'd they go?"

"Wouldn't say. Yes. I asked."

"And you're back," I stated the obvious. I set my things down on the couch beside him.

"I am. But not with good news. The vampire is lost. I'm sure of it. Nowhere to be found."

I nodded solemnly. It was what I'd come to expect. My heart ached for Cyrus. I wondered how I was going to deliver that news—or even if I should.

I went to the kitchen and made a cup of coffee. Gran was close to finishing her puzzle. It had slowly come together. I'd never offered any help. There were maybe thirty pieces left to go. Most of it was the sky in the background, every piece the same color and shape.

I sat there fiddling with them, happy when I found a piece that fit. I should've been doing this with her.

Gran was right about me—about me and Dave. I was using her house for sleep and not much else, spending the majority of my time elsewhere. We'd barely seen or talked to each other since Thanksgiving.

But that was her fault too. She hadn't told me what that spell in the graveyard was.

There was a knock at the front door. It was a suspiciously soft knock, timid. That meant it wasn't Dave or Trish. And not Gran. She would've came barging through.

I thought maybe it was a solicitor—how funny would that be after our interview with Hope Evans? Or maybe it was Agatha stopping by to finally have it out with Gran about the incident.

When I checked through the peephole, it was much worse. Much, much worse.

Who's there? Brad asked me in my head.

Magnified and stretched by the view from the peephole, the head bobbed in and out, revealing a red pixie cut and a long oval face, inches from the door.

"It's Summer Shields." I motioned to him. "Go upstairs. Get out of sight. I'll get rid of her."

My insides were squirming with a mixture of panic, trepidation, and something else. Something I couldn't put my finger on.

How does she do it?

How does she do what? Brad's voice popped into my head.

The computer, I thought. *She has to know it's here.*

So?

Long story. I'll explain later. Let me think.

I am.

No! Let me think with you out of my head. I swear I can feel you in here and it makes it so I can't think.

Two heads are better than one.

Not true. I pointed. "Get upstairs like I asked. That's an order."

Brad shrugged off the blankets, stretched lazily, and finally clambered up the stairs.

The knock came again, louder this time.

Think. Think. Think.

I'm just over here if you need me.

Get out of my head!

I yanked the door open and put myself between it and the jamb. My response to her showing up out of the blue was even more curt than Hope Evans's had been. I actually hoped the strain in my voice was evident. "Yes?"

"Hi," she said, her lips pushing upward to a smile—not her usual smirk or sneer, it was just as timid as the knock at the door.

"What do you want, Summer?"

"To talk. Nothing more, I promise."

"You came alone?"

She looked behind her. "It sure looks like it."

I rolled my eyes. "All right... I'm listening. Talk. You can't come in."

"No?"

"No," I said flatly. Her coming inside might trigger Gran's wards, or worse, it might let her through them. Permanently. I couldn't take a chance on either.

"But it's freezing."

"It's not freezing. You've got on a coat," I pointed out. "And a beanie. I'm sure you'll be all right."

"Fine. Okay. But can you at least come outside? This is kind of awkward."

"Sure. Let's go for a walk."

"These aren't exactly my walking boots." Summer indicated her footwear, her very muddy footwear.

"It looks like you've already been walking."

"Yeah, I guess I have. I'd like to sit down somewhere. Somewhere warm. A coffee would be nice."

I blinked, scolding myself for feeling a tiny bit of concern for Summer Shields.

Curses and cauldrons, Constance. She's just trying to use you.

I second that, Brad thought.

I rolled my eyes, mildly annoyed that the raccoon couldn't sense the gesture. "Give me a second. I'll bring you a thermos of coffee and we'll sit in my car. It has heated seats."

"That'd be great," Summer said.

I'd kind of been joking, but I'd made the offer, so...

A few minutes later, I thrust a travel mug into her hands and unlocked Prongs. She climbed in and I did the same, cranking the engine and setting our seats to warm. She trampled in mud, irritating me all the more. "What's this about? The computer? Jami's ParaTube videos?

"Sort of. I was in the neighborhood and remembered you lived here with your grandmother."

"That's right... I live here with my grandmother. For now... listen. Dave and I already looked in the computer. We couldn't find anything. I doubt you'd do better."

Summer disregarded that. "Constance, I didn't mean anything by what I said. It's not a big deal you live here and you're forty. It was just an observation. I remembered and I was in the—"

"Yeah. You already said that. You were in the neighborhood. I get it." But I questioned my own thinking. "Wait... what do you mean, you were in the neighborhood? What brought you here?"

"That's kind of the thing. I'm not sure. I could swear I was headed home from the studio, about to pull into my driveway when suddenly I was on your street."

"Yeah. That's odd."

"Don't you eat odd for breakfast?"

I smirked. "Is that what you think gives me my *witchy* powers?"

She smiled too. "You're a witch. Don't deny it. I haven't told Jade this but something's happening to me. I feel different. Strange. I kind of hoped you could tell me I wasn't going crazy."

"You aren't going crazy," I said. "Maybe something did lead you here. Maybe it means you *can* help with the laptop."

"Now you think I was drawn here to help you with the computer? Didn't you *just* say I wouldn't be able to help?"

I shrugged. "That was before I knew you were drawn here by magic and not some crazy hunch."

"Oh, so if it was a crazy hunch, you'd send me packing? But now I get to help."

"Something like that."

I tapped my seat warmer off and while my hand was up above the console, I reached out and touched Summer's wrist. Her magic sparked and sent a jolt through me.

"What are you—"

"Summer," I cut her off, "maybe you missed the part where I just admitted magic exists. It drew you here. I have it. Trish has it. And you have something like it too."

"You, uh, you touched me."

"Right... I just had to make sure it was true."

"Oh." She nodded, and for a second, she looked as if there might be something else she wanted to say to me. She swallowed it down. "Let me take the laptop and we can go from there."

21

SUMMONS

I let Summer take the laptop, with a promise she'd return it to Bewitched Books later in the day.

It was probably against the law. And it definitely was a breach of Dave's trust.

But what can it hurt? I reasoned.

Well, for one, Brad's voice echoed in my head, *if she's lying and she does find those videos, you're risking exposure of the paranormal world.*

It's her world now too.

She's an outsider, he pointed out. *She hasn't decided whether she wants in or out.*

You read her mind?

You told me to stay out of yours.

Yeah, well, next time, take the hint and stay out of both. I looked at the clock. *It's time to go to work.*

The car was still running. I backed out of the driveway. Brad's voice boomed again. *You should tell Trish about this. Tell her what's going on. She has a right to know that you're consorting with the enemy.*

Brad was right. He was always right. Familiars are great

as sounding boards but even better for advice. I hashed it out with Trish and she wasn't happy. I couldn't blame her. I felt icky about it as well.

"She's using you." Trish wouldn't meet my eyes. She fidgeted with the triquetra charm on her necklace.

"Maybe I'm using her."

"The likelihood of it being beneficial for both of you is not so high. Remind me again what you're getting out of this?"

I shrugged. "The videos Jami was making. There might be one about us."

"And you couldn't, maybe, let it go? Wouldn't it be better if it was never found?"

"I'd like to see it first."

Trish rolled her eyes. "I feel partially responsible for all this. I got your juices flowing the other day. But now you're being reckless."

"I'm not being reckless. Reckless would be interviewing suspects. Note, I haven't done that. I haven't gone near anyone besides Hope, if we count that—which I totally told Dave about."

"That reminds me. She has magic like Summer. I felt it. That's why I added her name to the list."

"Everyone in this town has hidden magic," I said.

"That's because this town hides magic. That's it! Hello—the mine. Maybe that's what this is all about... Jami probably questioned Hope about the mine."

I shook my head. "No. I read her book. Hope doesn't know any more about the mine than we do. She didn't put the puzzle together."

"But Jami did. Or someone who was helping her..."

"The boyfriend?"

Trish nodded.

"That's assuming there even is a puzzle," I said.

"It's Creel Creek. Come on. There's a puzzle. Or rather, a mine. We should interview him. See what he knows."

"Uh, no. Dave would kill me—if this guy didn't first. Plus, he has an alibi."

"They always do. Doesn't mean it's legit." Trish's green eyes danced. "What about the wife? Why don't we talk to her?"

"The same reason," I said. "Dave would get mad if I tried to do my own questioning. And what excuse do we have to talk to her? It's not like we can show up on her doorstep. 'Oh, hello, ma'am. We heard your husband might be a cold-blooded murderer. Want to sit down for coffee or tea and tell us all about it?'"

"You're right." Trish smiled. "Showing up on her doorstep for coffee doesn't make any sense. But what if she showed up here for coffee? That's not your fault, is it?"

"Depends." I shot Trish a skeptical look. I thought I knew where this was going. "Is she showing of her own free will?"

"She'll think that. And what Dave doesn't know…"

Before I could say anything else, Trish acted. She made a twisting gesture, as I'd seen her do with summoning spells, and said,

> "A cup of coffee, a cup of joe, a latte on the go.
> I summon her where over coffee she'll share…
> Truths and tales, with all the details,
> Of life and love, all of the above.
> I summon the wife, whatever her strife.
> From her husband's affair, she'll be happy to share."

"You shouldn't have done that."

"Want me to take it back?"

"Not really. But now I'm thinking why waste money on advertising when we could just do that..."

"Summon customers here? It wouldn't work. At least not like that. Not if we want their money."

"But it works for gossip?"

"No. It works for interviewing witnesses to a crime. Let's find out if she met Jami Castel in the library, like I think she did. And let's find out if her husband's been doing anything odd since this whole thing went down. That's always the problem with murderers, you know—they don't just sit tight and wait for things to blow over. In the end, they always do something to get themselves caught."

"You sound like an expert."

She shrugged and smiled. "I watch a lot of true crime."

◈

Once again, magic did its own thing. Trish's spell hadn't taken. No visitors showed that afternoon—not even Summer Shields.

Trish gave me an "I told you so" then locked up for the night.

My owl was a no show too. I waited beside the dumpster, searching the sky for her. But after ten minutes, she still hadn't appeared.

I had to lie to Dave about the whereabouts of Jami's laptop, claiming to have left it at Gran's house. It only made me feel worse about the other lies. So much worse that I gathered the girls into Allie's room for a chat.

"I think it's time we tell your dad about Licorice," I said.

"No! We can't!"

They begged. They pleaded. And finally, they cried.

I wasn't having it. The lies had added up so much that I had to come clean about one, at least, even if it was the most innocent of the lot.

I left them crying in Allie's room and asked Dave to follow me out to the garage. The problem—there was no cat to be found.

"What'd you need out here?" he asked.

"Nothing. Never mind. I thought I saw something out here." I searched high and low but found no hint of the little furball I'd been helping hide for weeks. The girls hid the food dish every night. They even scooped the old sandbox. There was no evidence a cat ever called the garage home.

When I returned to Allie's room, my news gave the girls even more to cry about.

~

THE NEXT MORNING, as usual, the shop was quiet. I took some of Trish's advice, sort of, and instead of a summoning spell, worked on a few social media ads.

I wasn't expecting instant success but after the ad was approved, a white Yukon slid into a parking space outside. A woman in a designer coat hopped out. She was brunette to gold ombre with shoulder length hair and oversize sunglasses. Her coat failed to hide the yoga pants she wore with her Ugg boots.

She walked past the window in the direction of the vape shop. She was out of sight for a moment but popped back in, sliding her sunglasses down her nose and peeking through the front window like she thought the store was closed.

She shrugged and came through the door.

I had a feeling I knew who this must be. I cursed Trish and magic, respectively.

"Um, this is weird," she held up her phone with my ad, "but do you do coffee drinks here? Like lattes?"

"We do," I said. "It's new."

"Oh. Okay then." She studied the espresso machine while I scurried from one counter to the other. "I guess I'll take a caramel macchiato. Upside down. Medium or grande or whatever."

"Coming right up." I took a marker and a medium cup. "Can I get a name?"

She looked around, a little baffled.

"It's for practice," I said. "One day we might have like two customers come in at the same time."

"What lofty aspirations. It's Emily—Emily Hart—spelled the normal way."

"Oh, it's way more fun for me if I guess." I smiled, jotting down **Normal Emily** on the cup. "How's your day been, Emily?" I asked and started grinding the beans.

"This morning was okay. It's bound to get better—I've got an appointment with a divorce lawyer this afternoon."

"Been there. Done that. Got the T-shirt."

"Really?"

"I think it was one-size-fits-all." I grimaced. "Cheating spouse."

"Me too! Then you'll understand how ridiculous it all is —how he, my husband—is trying to make it out like it's my fault. And my lawyer wants to compromise. My husband's a doctor. I think he can afford a little alimony."

"Or a lot," I said.

"Exactly! But the law in Virginia is tricky. Virginia is for lovers, not ex-lovers, apparently."

I couldn't have written the conversation and had it go

any better. That was magic doing what it does best. Trish's spell worked like a charm, so to speak.

I frothed Emily's milk, choosing my next words carefully. Emily hadn't yet paid. I finished her drink and set it on the counter beside the register.

"Can I ask you a personal question?"

"Shoot," she said.

"Did he come clean or did you figure it out?"

"Neither," Emily confirmed. "I found out from the police."

My eyes went wide, even though I knew this part of the story.

"Right? But don't worry." She waved it off. "He's not a criminal, just a poor judge of character."

"So, you had no idea?" I thought about my own experience. How I should've seen the warning signs. So many I'd disregarded.

"I mean, honestly, I guess I did. He works odd hours, so I never knew if he was supposed to be working or not. I started tracking his phone. But he'd turn it off, so I didn't know where he was."

"Never?"

She put her elbows on the counter and took a sip of the coffee, seeming satisfied. "Well, one time, I think he forgot. You'll never guess where he was."

I had a guess. I didn't voice it.

"He was at the library."

Bingo.

"The library?"

She nodded. "The next time his phone went off the grid, I went to the library. He wasn't there."

"Was anyone else there?" I asked, hoping I sounded nonchalant. "Anyone suspicious?"

She smiled. "Funny you should ask that because, yeah, his mistress was there. She just wasn't meeting him."

"Really?"

"She was meeting some older lady."

"Oh, wow," I said. "Did you know who it was?"

"No." She shrugged. "Just some old lady who drives a Buick."

22

ADMISSIONS AND OMISSIONS

I stood there gaping in stunned bewilderment.

Emily waved her hand in front of my face. "Are you all right? What do I owe you?"

I feigned a smile, feeling out of the moment.

"No, it's free today," I told her. "Sisters in solidarity. Good luck with the lawyer."

"Thank you." She held up her coffee in a salute. "And thanks for the coffee. It's fantastic."

My smile became genuine—I'd made a satisfactory latte. But the moment quickly faded, and a voice in my head screamed the words she'd said over and over again.

...some old lady who drives a Buick...

A lady who drives a Buick...

I followed Emily to the door, waving as she drove away. When her car was out of sight, I swung the placard to CLOSED and locked the door with a *click*.

"Is everything okay, Constance?" Twinkie was back, in her normal hideout near the register.

"It's not," I said. "I need to talk to someone."

"And it can't wait?"

I shook my head. I wasn't going to wait for Trish, not even for Summer Shields—should she actually make good on returning Jami's laptop today. No. This required my immediate attention.

I knew Gran was hiding something from me—from everyone—but I could never have imagined it was something this big.

The garage door was open and Gran's car—the Buick—was there, parked in the middle as usual, like it hadn't been anywhere the day before.

I wondered how many times I had made that assumption—how many times had she gone out without my knowledge?

More importantly, what had she been doing with Jami Castel?

I knew now, without a shadow of doubt, that Summer's hunch was true—that Jami's research revolved around us witches. And my own grandmother had been involved, perhaps even in Jami's death.

My blood ran cold at that thought.

The door nearly swung off its hinges when I went through. The opposite of a slamming door.

Startled, Gran sat up in her recliner, her hand raised, her finger pointed at the door like a gun. And it was loaded with magic.

"Oh, it's you."

"That's right. It's me. Expecting someone else?"

"I wasn't. Hence this." She swirled her pointer finger then used it to turn off the TV. "Shouldn't you be at work?

"I should be. But I came here for answers instead." I didn't know where to start so, I just came out with the accusation. "You had something to do with Jami's murder, didn't you?"

The color drained from Gran's face. She opened and closed her mouth a few times, likely trying to find the right words. This was not what I'd expected.

Gran was supposed to deny it. She wasn't supposed to be guilty. Not really. She was supposed to have some other explanation for why she talked to Jami Castel at the library.

Her lack of an answer was answer enough.

My knees almost buckled. I felt woozy and unable to stand. I made it to the couch and scooted Brad over. He was asleep next to Stevie. Gran had obviously done something to them. There was no way they would sleep through something like this.

"This is a private conversation." Her voice was a whisper, and her eyes welled up with tears. "A conversation between me and my successor."

"Your what?"

"I already told you I was guilty," she said softly.

"No, you didn't."

"I did. I told you to cuff me." She held up her wrists and I remembered the conversation.

"No. You were joking. I thought you were joking."

"That's the thing about jokes—there's usually a hint of truth in them, sometimes more."

"Gran." My voice sounded even more strained than hers. "Tell me you didn't murder someone."

"I didn't murder anyone."

"Then... then what happened?"

"A spell," she said. "A spell gone wrong."

"Explain. Please." My head was spinning.

"You had that book the other day, the book about the mine. It's true—there is a hidden mine in Creel Creek, and it doesn't contain coal or silver. It's a source of magic. Pure magic."

The first question that popped into my brain wasn't about the murder. "Where is it?"

"It's best if you don't know," Gran said. "It's better for everyone not to know."

"Why?"

Gran answered my question with a question of her own. "Do you remember what my maiden name was?"

I realized I didn't. If we'd been closer when I was growing up, I'd have known.

"No." I shook my head.

"You've never asked why I settled here after your grandfather's passing."

That was also true. I only knew she'd moved here from Florida. "I thought because of the magic here—because of the paranormal community..."

"It was the magic," she said. "More accurately, the magic mine. My maiden name is Creel. My mother was a witch. But my father had a secret of his own. He was tasked with being the guardian of the magical mine, just as you have."

"I haven't been—" I couldn't finish the words, realizing what that stunt in the graveyard must have been. She'd transferred this duty to me. She'd tricked us. She made sure it was only my hand on that tree. "What do you mean by guardian?"

"You understand that we—witches—get our magic from within?"

I nodded.

"There are others who don't—others who can only sense the presence of magic."

"Right. They're sensitive. I get it." Trish had said it about Jami. And about Summer.

"Do you understand how they *can* wield magic? They can use it if they take it or if they find it."

"Like in the mine?"

"Like in the mine." Her eyes went to Stevie and Brad, conked out beside me. "It's imperative that the familiars know nothing about this, as they could wield this magic too. Their inability to use magic on Earth is part of what keeps them in check, so to speak. It keeps the balance from tipping."

"I don't understand."

"I'm trying to explain…"

She was trying to, but it wasn't what I wanted to hear. My questions tumbled out. "But what does this have to do with Jami's murder? Did she find the mine? Is that why you killed her?"

Gran rubbed her temples. "It's not that simple, Constance. The charge isn't to guard the mine from these people or even to keep the magic inside it. The magic is there for everyone, but there's only so much.

"A long time ago, a man thought he could take it for his own and dole it out as he saw fit. He even brought our ancestor in on the scheme."

"Okay…"

"The mine—the magic—had a mind of its own."

"The explosion," I said.

"Melvin Creel realized his mistake. Since that time, we've been protecting the mine and the people from such an event. When the task fell to me, I cast a simple spell. It allows a person to procure enough for their needs—and only their needs. Should they try to take more, more magic than they ought to, the mine will kick them out with a warning. Should they try again…"

"They die?"

She locked eyes with me and nodded. "It only ever happened one other time."

"Steven Robillard?" I guessed.

She nodded again.

"But that doesn't make sense," I said. "Why would you put them out on display like that? Is that why you talked to Jami at the library? Did you try to warn her?"

"Slow down," Gran said. "I didn't put those bodies on display!"

"You didn't?"

"No. But the magic flowed out of me when the death happened. I felt it in the pit of my stomach. Then you got that phone call the next day. And I've been trying to figure out who set them up that way and why ever since."

"Why didn't you tell me then? I could've helped you."

"I was afraid you wouldn't understand. It was my spell. My fault. I should've changed it after that Robillard fellow. I knew then there were other ways to protect the mine, but I never changed it. I thought it was over."

"And what about Jami? When you warned her?"

Gran shook her head. "I'm not sure what you're talking about. I never spoke to her."

"But there was someone in a Buick at the library," I said.

Gran continued to shake her head. "Plenty of other people drive Buicks, Constance."

This didn't make any sense. If it wasn't Gran who spoke to Jami, then who was it and why? I had so many questions. But my next was probably least important. "Where were you yesterday... when you were gone?"

"Putting together the puzzle," Gran said.

I sat up. "What do you mean?"

"I was returning your library book and doing some digging of my own."

My eyes shot to the stack of cardboard boxes beside the front door, boxes from all the online ordering she did—

boxes that I hadn't yet recycled. I'd set my copy of *Unexplained Disasters* there, meaning to return it.

It wasn't there. In its place was a silver laptop.

"Yes. Your friend dropped that off last night."

"She's not my friend." Summer Shields. At least she kept her word. I wondered if she'd found the videos on it and if she'd released them to the world without my knowledge.

"Either way," Gran said, "she needs to speak to you."

"That's all she said?"

"That's all."

"Okay. But back to the puzzle. What were you doing at the library?"

"A bit of digging, so to speak. A good deal of reading. I believe that author knows more than she's letting on—more than she wrote in the book. In fact, I'm willing to bet she knows everything."

~

Hope Evans was more reluctant to let us in this time.

"Sorry," she said, "it's just this deadline and I'm really supposed to be writing. I don't have the time to—"

"You'll make time," Gran said with a swoop of her finger. The door jerked open, much to the surprise of Hope Evans.

Gran strode inside, as confident as ever, and sat down on the spacious couch in Hope's living room. There were no niceties. No faux interview either. Gran settled down to business.

"I know about you," she said.

"What? You know about my books?"

"No. I know how you research your books."

This seemed to cause Hope some discomfort. "I do a lot of research. I, um, use online databases, journals—"

"You speak to the dead," Gran said.

Hope gulped. "What?" she denied. "You can't believe I—"

Gran wiggled her fingertips and a flame burst out, lighting the fireplace under Hope's TV, which was meant to use gas.

Hope gulped again. "You're a witch."

"We both are," Gran agreed.

"Oh. I should've known."

"And you're a necromancer," Gran said.

"It's not that simple. I wanted to do more. I hoped I could do more. But it's all I'm capable of doing."

"Who did you talk to about the mine?"

She nodded as if she knew this question was coming. "Several of the men from the explosion."

"Did they lead you to it?"

"They did," she said. "I went inside. But it kicked me out almost as soon as I was in. I'd already taken my fill."

I had questions but Gran was running this show. She pressed on. "And this new book, what's it about? Who did you speak to while you *researched*?"

Hope faltered. "It was supposed to be about mysterious deaths. Suicides that weren't, things like that. I talked to Steven Robillard. But I think you know that."

Things were falling into place.

"He got you thinking about the mine again, didn't he?"

"Yes. But no." She turned to me with pleading eyes. "It's not what you think. I swear, it's not. I had nothing to do with Jami's death. Nothing. I thought my research and hers were unrelated."

"So, you did see her prior to her death?" I asked.

"No. No." She steadied herself and took a breath. "We emailed. We bounced ideas back and forth. She told me about a story she was working on—I was hoping she could help me with something I was intrigued by."

"Go on," Gran said.

"She sent me these pictures from the vineyard, taken decades apart over a century or so. I knew immediately it was a story I could do something with. I could help her. Or I could use it for a book… if she let me."

"And she wouldn't?" I jumped to the conclusion.

"We never got to talk about it."

"What did you give her?" Gran asked.

"Something nowhere near as good, or so I thought. There's this couple in my neighborhood. The wife, she comes over every now and then. We chat, mostly she talks about her troubles and things. She believed her husband was cheating on her. I think she knew I'm the type to stare out my window while I'm procrastinating."

"Is her name Emily?"

"Yes. How did you—"

"Don't worry about it," Gran dismissed it. "Go on."

"Okay. This is where things get strange. Her husband kept going off. But he wasn't cheating on her. He kept going up near the mine. I followed him one day, but I couldn't keep up. And I can't set foot in that mine again. I thought Jami could take up the mantle—see what he was really up to. I never thought it would lead to her death."

"No, you thought you'd protect your own interests first." Gran blamed herself. That was written plainly on her face.

"I have a quick question," I said. "How does necromancy work?"

Hope hesitated. "Well, it's all about the life after death. Reanimations are harder to pull off but tend to work better than any attempt to contain a ghost. You need a suitable vessel to host any spirit."

"I'll stop you there." Gran put a finger out. A loaded finger. "You'll be letting Mr. Caulfield leave of his own volition straightaway."

"I will do that." Hope nodded energetically. "He's free to go," she said to no one.

Her head jerked toward the dining room, and she scanned the ceiling. We followed her gaze, but his spirit didn't pass near us. He'd probably poofed away to the vineyard.

"Another thing," I said. "Can you tell me what was in the fourth photo? The photo without the vineyard's owner?"

"Fourth photo?" Hope looked perplexed.

I dug it out of my purse and passed it to her.

For a moment, she looked startled. "Oh, well, that's me and my babysitter, Agatha Sundwick."

23

IN WITCH WE CLOSE IN

Bewitched Books became a makeshift headquarters or at least a meeting place for the parties involved. It was less conspicuous than Gran's house, given its proximity to Agatha's, and less formal than Dave's office.

He and Mac rode together and met us along with Trish and Cyrus. Mr. Caulfield's ghost loitered near the back room, visible only to us witches and Cyrus.

"I told you it wasn't a normal murder," I said.

"And I told you the other body was a prop. Guess we were both right."

"That's such a man thing to say." Trish rolled her eyes.

"It's technically true," I agreed with Dave. "Unless we can prove otherwise."

Dave tipped his ball cap with a finger. "Proof. I'm not hearing much. Nothing I could bring her in on. And I'm fuzzy on the details. Why would Agatha be involved, isn't she a witch?"

"We're not sure," I said. "Trish needs to get near her to see if maybe she's been faking it somehow."

Trish agreed. "I don't think she's let me near her since I

received the gift. I think maybe she knows I'll figure her out, whatever she is."

"And that could be?" Dave asked the obvious question.

"Any number of things," Gran said mournfully.

"She could be possessed," I said, having had dealings with demons.

"Could be. Or a familiar gone rogue."

"Is that why you put Twinkie to sleep?" Trish asked, and Gran nodded.

Trish hadn't been keen on that idea and looked equally as put out about it now.

"Are we forgetting anything?" Cyrus put in. "Like that maybe she was being blackmailed too? You said there was a picture of her."

Dave nodded. "But that picture, it's not exactly proof of anything."

"Okay. What's the plan?" Trish asked.

Dave took off the cap and raked a hand through his hair. "I can't exactly get a warrant for something like this. Magical murder requires magical investigation. And I didn't think there was magic involved in the death."

"You're right," I said. "I couldn't find a trace of it at the scene."

"That's odd," Trish said.

Gran shrugged.

"Anyway, I'll let you three take point with me or Mac, if necessary."

"We could search her house," I offered. "We might find some link to the murders there. Or maybe we do surveillance? I don't know. These ideas sound kind of stupid when I say them out loud."

"There are no wrong answers," Dave said. "And I hate to play devil's advocate here—I don't know a lot about magic—

but wouldn't she have wards to protect her house? Has anyone here been invited inside?"

We all shook our heads. Not even Gran had been invited into Agatha's house. That was kind of suspicious. But given their relationship, not that big a surprise.

The door chimed and Summer Shields was in the doorway with a horrified look on her face. She hadn't expected this crowd.

"Yes?" Dave asked her.

"I, uh, I came to see Constance."

This was bad. Dave didn't know about the laptop. I was going to be in trouble for sure. But given the circumstances, how close we were to finally nabbing Jami's killer, I thought it best to put it out in the open.

"Whatever you have to say," I said, "you can say it in front of everybody."

She blinked, taking everything—everyone—in. "I found the videos."

"You found them?" Dave's gaze bounced from her to me and back again. "Where did you find them? Can you show us?"

"They were on the laptop," Summer said. "Hidden."

"Where is the laptop?" Dave's question was for me.

"At Gran's," I answered.

"It doesn't matter," Summer cut in. "They're gone now. Disappeared, as if they were never there."

"How?" Dave growled.

"I, uh, I don't know," she said. "One second they were there and the next, I couldn't find them."

"Then tell us what you saw." It was Trish, and her voice had the edged tone she reserved for Summer and Jade.

"They weren't what I thought they'd be..."

"No?"

"They were videos of that guy—the guy I thought was her boyfriend. I don't think he was her boyfriend. I think she was helping him somehow."

"Helping him do what?"

"I don't know." Summer shrugged. "They weren't like, good videos. He was just out in the woods, walking."

"To the mine," Gran said.

Dave nodded. "So, he lied to us about Jami. Let's put some eyes on him, Mac. But don't spook him. And let's not bring him in until we know more about Agatha and her role in these events. They're probably working together." He leveled his gaze on Summer. "Anything else, Miss Shields?"

She shook her head.

Trish cleared her throat. "So, is this a plan or a plan to make a plan?"

"I think I've got an idea," I answered.

"We'll hear you out once the reporter leaves," Dave said. "And separately, we'll discuss the situation with the laptop."

I winced. He looked pretty mad.

"I guess that's my cue." Summer slinked toward the door.

Feeling sorry for her, and guilty about the lies and everything else, I followed, catching her on the sidewalk outside. Even though all eyes were on us, I knew they couldn't hear what I was going to say to her.

"Thank you, Summer," I said. "You did the right thing."

"I wasn't going to release them anyway," she said. "Even if they were what I wanted. I wasn't going to. You probably don't believe me."

"I do."

I believed her.

~

Gran hated my plan.

This was because it hinged on using Brad, and as guardian, she wanted the familiars as far removed from the mine as possible. But that wasn't how I wanted to play my guardian role. I trusted Brad.

I attempted to explain without mentioning the mine.

Outside Gran's house, I explained to Brad we'd found Mr. Caulfield here on Earth, locked away in bone china by a necromancer. I also explained the relationship between Hope and Agatha.

He had questions.

"I'm not following why Agatha would do such a thing… does she keep tabs on this woman? How'd she know about the unearthed body?"

"The body wasn't a big secret," I said. "She probably talked to Griffin Barber."

The raccoon stared blankly.

"You know, the cemetery guy…"

"Oh, right. You made me stay in the car for that one."

I nodded, continuing, "It's possible that Jami was blackmailing Agatha somehow. We need you to look in her house for proof."

"Sneak into a witch's house?" His paws went together in a warming motion, almost like that raccoon meme. "You do realize that's all you had to say, right?"

I grinned. "Then let's do it."

The good thing about my plan was Dave was comfortable with it. He knew that, if it came down to it, I could hold my own against Agatha, at least until the cavalry arrived.

The cavalry was parked on the dirt path behind the cemetery—the same place we'd found Jami's car. Things were adding up quickly. We just needed these last pieces of the puzzle.

Brad hid. I stretched. And along came Agatha in her usual turquoise track suit, nylon swishing.

I waved and power walked to join her. Brad snuck through the neighborhood to her house.

"Do you mind if I join you today?" I asked.

She barely acknowledged me. "It's a free road."

I'm in position, Brad thought.

Just a minute. We're coming around the corner by her house.

I scanned her front yard, the crawl space under her porch, and the rock garden for Brad, satisfied when I didn't find him out in the open.

Agatha hadn't even given the house a glance, focusing on the road ahead.

Minor problem. How am I getting inside?

Look at this neighborhood, I thought. *I bet it's unlocked.*

Yes. But height is an issue.

Climb up the potted plant on her porch. If it's locked, check under it for the key.

A few seconds passed then Brad thought, *I'm in.*

We knew her house was warded. I'd checked this morning when she started her walk, finding the door thrummed with magic.

If I had tried to barrel through, her wards would've done a number on me. What, I couldn't be sure. But the few times I'd seen wards in action weren't pretty.

Possibly, I could've spelled a shield around me. Magic being unpredictable and following its own sort of rules, there was a chance my magic might outdo hers—our need for the truth would trump her need for privacy in her home.

But Agatha had years of experience to my less than a year.

"So, you're sticking to the neighborhood today."

"I am." My heart beat faster, remembering she'd been out on her walk when I'd discovered Jami's car.

Don't serial killers usually return to the scene of their crime? Do they? Brad questioned.

I realized that Agatha was going to spot this lie.

"Why's that?" she asked. "Aren't you usually a runner?"

"It's, uh, my calf. I pulled something the other day." Lying wasn't my gift, but at least I'd prepared this one. "I thought I should take it easy today."

"Easy, huh? I won't be slowing my pace on your account. I'm sorry if you can't keep up."

What a sweetheart.

Serial killer, sweetheart, she sure is something, Brad though. *And she sure has a thing for cock.*

"What? Come again?" I sputtered, the words flying from my mouth.

Cock. You know, roosters. The house is decorated with them. Figurines everywhere, an oven mitt, and the kitchen towels. Ewww...

Agatha's eyes narrowed. But she kept her pace up and her arms pumping. "I said if you can't keep up, then you shouldn't bother."

False alarm, Brad thought. *The wallpaper in the guest bathroom. There's a rooster playing a lute. That reminds me. Should I take up an instrument? Is a raccoon playing the banjo too on the nose?*

Brad. Focus. You have to find something.

"I won't slow you down," I assured Agatha but feigned a slight limp all the same.

You're sure she doesn't have a familiar?

Just a cat, I think.

There's the food dish. Eightball. What a name. Why hasn't it come out to greet me?

Cats are skittish, I thought. *It's probably hiding.*
Unlike familiars. We're not skittish at all. Oh, there she is.
Agatha pumped through another turn.
The cat? I asked. *It's there?*
Yes. That's odd, indeed.
What is?
Its thoughts, he said. *It reminds me of that owl.*

We were on Agatha's street again. And I was sure we were going to pass her house and do another loop. So sure, in fact, that she was halfway up her lawn by the time it registered that she was heading inside.

Abort. I thought hard. *Abort! Abort!*

"You're done for the day?" I called to her.

"I think so. Yes. It was good seeing you. And tell your grandmother I said hello. But do tell her I won't be seeing her on the solstice. I have *other* plans."

"Oh?"

She didn't elaborate. She spun and headed for her door, marching through the grass and over the rock garden.

The rock garden!

The evidence wasn't inside the house. It was right there in front of us, in front of her house, the whole time.

24

IN WITCH AN ARM BREAKS

With the girls out of school for the Christmas holidays, Dave was short-staffed at home. He'd usually be taking these days off with them, and it was unfair to keep asking so much of Imogene.

I didn't mind watching them while he went to work. There were a few things left to do, then he could close the books on the murder investigation.

He knew a paranormal-friendly lawyer in the Creek County Attorney's office willing to hear what he'd gathered about Agatha. After that, there'd be special proceedings, with jurors familiar with the supernatural.

That was sometime in the future. Today, he was waiting for the go ahead, so he could serve the warrant for Agatha's arrest.

And he wouldn't have to worry much about her potential use of magic, thanks to the moon talisman necklace given to him by the shifters at the League Den. Dave could transform into his werewolf form almost anytime. And in wolf form, he was basically invulnerable to spells. Plus, he had shifters like Mac with similar supernatural defenses at his disposal.

It would be quite the show if Agatha decided not to go quietly. For me, there wasn't much left to do. There was nothing to do, really. Nothing to do but think.

There were some minor details I wanted to iron out. I wanted to know more about Agatha's cat, almost as much as I wanted to know about my owl. Or rather, the owl. It wasn't mine and I hadn't seen it for weeks.

There was also the guy—Jami's non-boyfriend, Hope's neighbor, Emily's husband, and maybe Agatha's accomplice.

Dave had never told me his alibi, just that it was solid, and their surveillance had uncovered nothing of consequence, nothing tying the man to Agatha. Well, nothing aside from Jami and her videos which they didn't have.

My fault... maybe.

I ruminated on things while the girls played outside. From the living room, I watched as they ran around the yard, Kacie trailing the other two by a good distance.

Aside from a few squabbles that morning and their terrible taste in television, they were barely an inconvenience.

Hmm.

What had also been barely an inconvenience was my interview with Emily. The interview had basically spurred the investigation in the right direction. And I hadn't gone out of my way for it.

Granted, Gran could've come clean a lot sooner.

I knew I should allow Dave to tie up this loose end. But he had so much on his plate already. The more I thought about it, the more I thought how easy it'd be to help.

Making him come to me seemed like the obvious choice.

I could remember, almost verbatim, the spell Trish had used to summon Emily.

Except I wasn't at Bewitched Books. Dave's house was far from a casual stop.

I muttered a spell that should cause us to meet. Then I waited for the magic to do its work.

"Constance! Constance! Constance!" The calls came from the sliding door to the back porch. Allie and Kacie were jumping up and down, eyes wide. They yelled my name more times than that, and there were other words mixed in, indecipherable. Their pleas grew louder but less distinct.

I slid the door open. "What's going on? One at a time, please."

"Come on," Allie said hurriedly. "Come on. She's back. She's back!"

"Who's back? Where's Elsie?"

"Licorice," they yelled in unison.

Allie took my hand and tugged.

Kacie ran ahead, down the steps, and into the yard. Dave's house was on half an acre, most of which was surrounded by a privacy fence lined with shrubs. There was a small playset with a slide and two trees, one much taller than the other.

It was cold, but there was no snow on the ground, and the girls were in jackets with beanies covering their heads.

I scanned the yard and the playset for Elsie. My heart lurched when I couldn't find her. I wrenched my arm from Allie's grip and cupped both hands around my mouth. "Elsie!"

"Elsie!" Allie called. "Have you got her?"

"Up here!" The words came from the smaller of the two trees, with other sounds as well.

"You got her?" Allie ran ahead.

"Almost!"

In true cat fashion, Licorice was stuck on the second highest branch, meowing like mad—acting as if she had no clue how she got there and even less of a clue how she would get down.

A few branches below her, Elsie's feet were nestled in the crook of a large branch. With one arm, she clung to a small branch. The other stretched upward, her eyes fixed on the cat and not paying much attention to what that branch in her hand was doing. It bent almost in half as Elsie stretched, desperately reaching out to Licorice.

SNAP!

The branch broke and she was falling. It happened so fast. One second she was in the tree, the next, she was on the ground. She wasn't even crying. At first, I thought nothing was wrong.

"Ow," she cried out. "Ow."

"What is it? What hurts?"

"My arm," she said.

She struggled up to a sit without using it. In the jacket, it looked fine. I helped her shrug it off and found it was definitely not fine.

The blood drained from her face. I had to do something. With magic on my brain, I went there first.

> "Mend the bone,
> as hard as stone."

It didn't work.

There was still a small knot where the arm bent at an odd angle. A bruise was forming under the skin.

It wasn't my best effort at a spell. I wasn't thinking clearly. Either was she.

Elsie had gone from child in pain to stoic calm. Her eyes glazed over, focused on the spot between her wrist and elbow where things weren't as they should be.

She was in some shock.

"Elsie," I said softly, "I need you to focus on me. You're going to be fine. This is nothing. You'll get a cast and all the ice cream you can eat. Oh, no. Maybe that's for tonsils. Still, you'll get a cool cast."

I was no longer thinking about magic. I'd tried. I'd failed. It was probably something to do with need—why magic a bone back together when I could so easily speed to the ER and have a doctor do it?

Magic sucks...

"Girls, let's get to the car. Quickly, please!"

Dave's white minivan was parked in the middle of the driveway. I got behind the wheel yet again, but this time the pedal never left the floorboard.

I called Dave on the way to the hospital. Funny enough, it was he who had to console me. Elsie was in the middle row, holding her broken arm with the other and putting on a brave face.

"Constance, it's okay," he said. "This stuff happens all the time. They're kids."

"No. It's always on my watch." My vision blurred as tears formed in my eyes. All I needed was to cause a wreck.

"Not always."

"I'm not sure I'm cut out for this," I said without thinking.

"Constance..."

A red-hot tear plummeted down my cheek.

"What was she doing?"

"Climbing a tree," I said. "The cat got—"

"The what?"

"Uh, never mind," I said, realizing my error. "You'll meet us there, right?"

"I'll be there as fast as I can," Dave said. "We've got a few things to wrap up first." His voice took on a softer tone. "Sweetheart—Elsie—you're gonna be fine. Constance is gonna take great care of you. The doctor will too."

Dave called Imogene and she managed to show up just as I had all the paperwork filled out.

For half a second, I thought she was going to offer to go back with Elsie. Instead, she kept the other two while I went through the big emergency room doors with the scared little girl.

We were both scared.

Elsie was seen by a nurse and had x-rays done.

We sat there waiting for what felt like an extremely long time before the doctor strode casually into the room. A nurse came in behind him with a cart.

With no sense of urgency, he looked at a folder he'd retrieved from a box outside the door.

Come on, I thought. *Can't you see this girl's in pain! Where has he been for the last fifteen minutes?*

I knew full well he was likely busy with other emergencies, some of which were equally as pressing as a broken arm. Some life-threatening.

"I heard we had a little fall," the doctor said. "I'm Doctor Hart. I'm here to fix you up."

Doctor Hart. Like Emily Hart. Like the husband that I'd so wanted to talk to and used magic to bring us together.

Elsie's broken arm—it was *all* my fault.

25

IN WITCH IT'S ALL MY FAULT

The procedure didn't take very long—if it could even be called a procedure. There was no operation. Elsie was given a local anesthetic, a shot which drew the most screams, then Doctor Hart maneuvered the bone into place.

I held Elsie's other hand, and the doctor and the nurse fitted her with a temporary cast.

I couldn't speak the whole time. There was no chitchat, no interviewing him. I was as numb as Elsie's broken arm. I think the nurse asked me a few questions. Possibly, I answered. And I was screaming inside.

We were there because of my magic. My words—my intentions—had failed me yet again. Elsie was in this pain because of me.

Dave rushed in after it was over. He looked tired and weary, frazzled, much worse than he had that morning leaving for work. I guessed his children getting injured did that to him.

What did he ever see in me?

Dave only had eyes for Elsie. He wrapped her in a hug, kissing her forehead. "How are you, baby girl?"

"Fine. Constance said I'll get ice cream."

"Ice cream for sure. You know, I believe you're going to get that cat now too."

"Really?"

"Anything," Dave said. "Whatever you want."

"She needs to see the orthopedic surgeon," Doctor Hart cut in. "If it's set right, he'll put on a more permanent cast."

Dave took in the doctor. His eyes widened. "Doctor Hart," he said, regaining his composure slightly. "I was just about to call you."

"You were?"

Dave's jaw tightened. "We need to talk."

The doctor faltered. "I'm kind of busy right now…"

Dave shook his head and guided Elsie toward the door. "Constance, could you take her out to Imogene and come back?"

"Of course."

"You realize who this is, right?"

"I do."

"Go now." Dave led the girl to me, and Elsie took my hand.

"I can't just—"

"You'll listen to me right now," Dave interrupted. "I thank you for straightening my girl's arm out. But now, it's my turn. There are several things I need to get straight, so to speak."

The nurse was there, a balding man, looking confused and troubled. "Should I inform the charge nurse?"

Doctor Hart nodded. And I took Elsie out to the rest of her family. I returned a minute later, not quite as puzzled as the nurse but curious why Dave now considered a chat with the doctor so important.

Dave was asking, "... your shift started earlier this morning?"

"It's a ten-hour shift," the doctor said. "I believe I'm on hour eight right now."

Satisfied, Dave pressed on. "Why did you allow us to believe Jami Castel was your mistress? And I understand you let your wife do the same."

"How do you—"

"It's not important how we know. Right now, I need the truth. It's imperative you tell us everything."

The doctor sank into the chair I'd been sitting in and buried his face in his hands. "It seemed like the easiest explanation. You assumed and I went with it."

"But why? If it wasn't the truth, I can only assume what really happened is much worse..."

"It is," the doctor said. "So much worse."

"Do you want your lawyer?" Dave asked.

"No. I don't need my lawyer, not for this."

"Tell us what happened."

He lifted his chin and instead of looking at Dave, he found me. "I was losing my memory. Not just that. It was like there were segments of time that I lost. I'd start going one place and end up in another."

I knew too much about things like this. It was obvious that Doctor Hart had been possessed.

"And Jami," I asked, "where does she come in?"

"She offered to help me," he said. "I don't know how she knew what was going on. But she approached me, and I took her up on the offer. The way things were happening, it was like clockwork. I pretty much knew when and where my memory was going to fail. I just couldn't prevent it, ya know? Jami took a video of it."

"And what did she find?" Dave asked.

"I went out into the woods. She lost me in there. When I came back, I was carrying some rocks. I dropped them off, she took them, I came to, and she showed me the video. That was that."

"Why didn't you tell us this before?"

"Because I'm a doctor. I thought I was going crazy. I would lose everything if this came to light." He returned to his feet, quickly—a little too quickly. Dave's hand went to his holster. "But it's okay. I'm better now. I haven't had a memory lapse since that day. Whatever Jami did, it worked."

"Jami didn't do anything," I said.

"Not true," Dave countered. "Jami talked to Agatha that day. And we found those rocks in her car. The two are linked."

"Agatha?" Doctor Hart looked perplexed. "Who's she?"

"She's our suspect," I told him. "Dave's gathering evidence for a warrant."

"No," Dave said softly. "There's no need for a warrant. This morning, Agatha Sundwick didn't come out for her usual walk. Mac performed a wellness check. Agatha Sundwick is dead."

26

FOR A CAT

It felt odd being in Agatha's house. Her body was found lying on the living room rug beside the coffee table. There was a rooster coffee cup on the table, half full of black coffee, over a day old now with a numbered tag next to it.

I wondered if this meant we were wrong about her. Or right. Did she manipulate Jami and cause her death? Did someone else?

And did Agatha die of natural causes?

She had been up to something, that was a certainty, but had it been murder or was she just a pawn in this too?

There were no other leads.

I walked into Agatha's kitchen. Everything in order, nothing out of place. I stepped over the cat's dish beside her refrigerator.

"Dave," I called into the next room. "What happened to the cat?"

He popped into the kitchen and said, "What cat?"

I read the name on the food dish out loud, "Eightball."

Agatha had come to the store the same day as Jade and

Summer. It was barely a blip on my radar, given other events. We'd talked about her cat.

"I can ask Mac about it," Dave said. "He might've left the door open yesterday. If it was here and got out..."

"That's odd," I said.

"What is?"

"The cats."

Licorice was also gone. We'd returned to Dave's house to find the tree empty. No cat in the garage. We scoured the whole neighborhood looking for her. The girls were devastated... again.

"Eightball," I said. "Isn't that a name for a black cat?"

"You think they're the same cat?"

"Ask again later."

"Was that a Magic 8 Ball joke?"

"A bad one," I said. "I'm going to talk to Gran about it."

"You want a ride?" he asked.

"No."

"You sure?" Out the kitchen window, a light snow had begun to fall but nothing was sticking... yet.

"It's a short walk."

He nodded. "I'll be over there in just a bit."

I zipped up my coat, threw the hood over my hair, and started down the street, doing an Agatha-style power walk against the chill in the air and the small flakes of snow blurring my vision.

I was close to Gran's house when a black cat raced across my path. It wound between my legs and arched its back. I couldn't tell if it was trying to kill me or if it was happy to see me.

"Are you the villain in this story?" I asked it.

I tried to pick it up, but it scampered into the neighbor's yard in the direction of the woods.

I got out my phone and called Dave. "I found the cat."

"You did? Where are you?"

"At Gran's."

"Keep it there."

"I'll try. I haven't caught it."

"Don't go anywhere," Dave said. "I'll be right there. It could be dangerous."

He was right. It could be. It could be whatever killed Agatha. It could be a person; Brad said its thoughts were like the owl's.

And like the owl, my spell to transform it did nothing. Nothing except drive it away.

"Here, kitty, kitty. Come back."

The cat went farther into the woods.

"I can't go with you. Dave says to stay put."

The snow was falling harder now, swirling in the wind, sticking to the ground.

I followed the cat a little. I wasn't far from the road. And when Dave got there, he'd be able to see me.

The cat yowled in my direction then disappeared into the trees.

I was of two minds. The cat was either luring me to my death or this was some sort of *Lassie* scenario. It needed my help. There was no in-between.

There was no telling if she'd come back for me or keep going. And no telling if I'd find her again, not in the woods with snow falling.

I tried not to think about Elsie. After all, if this cat was innocent, this would be how many times I'd prevented the two from being together?

Also, my gut said the cat was okay.

Brad! I thought hard. He could help. He could follow the cat for me.

No answer.

My owl wasn't here to help me either.

I was on my own until Dave got here. I called him again.

"You have it?" he answered.

"No. Where are you?"

"I'll be a few more minutes," he said.

"She's getting away," I told him.

"Sit tight. I'll be—"

"I'll be right behind Gran's house," I said, jogging to the spot I'd last seen the cat. "Trust me, okay?"

"Just stay on the phone," he said. "If you stay on the phone, you can go. I've got Find My Friends."

"Okay."

The cat hadn't been waiting. I saw her well ahead of me, tail up high, pawing the light snow. Her head twisted when she heard me, and she paused. Her eyes were asking me to follow a little farther, not to give up.

"Kitty," I pleaded. "Where are you going? Didn't you like it with those girls? They'll spoil you."

She wasn't hearing it. She kept going. She reached a path—the path to the graveyard—and followed it.

"You got her?" Dave asked.

"Almost," I lied.

I was fine as long as we stuck to the path. I knew it well enough. She kept going, with me trailing several feet behind her.

She ran up the hill, stopping where the path forked. Only I never knew it forked like that.

I began to feel a prickly sensation on my neck. I was being watched—I was sure of that—but I'd had this feeling in the corn maze, the day Elsie chased this cat. A day later, two bodies were found. That couldn't be a coincidence.

Had the cat really just led me to my death? Or was something else afoot?

A foot.

Beside the cat, on the path that led elsewhere, there was a shoeprint in the snow. A fresh shoeprint.

"They've found it," I said to the phone.

"Who? Found what?"

"The mine," I said.

The cat bobbed its head. It turned tail and headed down the path.

"How? Constance, I'm at your Gran's house now. Where are you?"

That was reassuring. Dave wasn't far. He could track me here. It'd be easy.

I set off behind her, feeling confident, feeling like the story was coming to a close. I was about to tell him as much when a branch swung into the path ahead of me.

For a moment, it was all I could see—the large branch coming at me like a baseball bat. Then a blinding pain in my forehead sent me sprawling backward. I landed on the hard, uneven ground.

The lights went out.

27

IN WITCH I'M BURIED ALIVE

I woke up short of breath. I couldn't tell if it was a minute or several hours later. The world had gone dark. And cold.

My head throbbed with pain. So much so, I was thankful there was no light wherever I was.

It smelled earthy. I could barely move. I was somewhere confining. I felt around, finding things all around me. They felt hard like rock. But some were brittle, brittle like bone.

Bone.

I groped the objects beside me. A ribcage. A skull beside my head.

"Hello." A wave of heebie-jeebies went down my spine.

I had a good feeling, a hunch, that I was in a coffin. I pushed on the lid to no avail. Either it had some sort of locking mechanism, which was possible, or more likely, hundreds—if not thousands—of pounds of dirt had been shoveled atop my prison.

Several things came to mind. Was I in the graveyard? Or the cemetery? Had whoever knocked me out and shoved me in a casket left a trail for Dave to follow?

Had Gran been right—was it Griffin Barber all along? He seemed the type to use coffins for getting rid of someone.

The only air available was what was inside with me. It was being sucked up fast. I was breathing so hard. I had to get my nerves under control.

And I really had to stop getting myself into situations like this. A problem for another time. I hoped.

At least this time I had full control of my body. But while my arms and my legs weren't bound, there was little they could do. Clawing and kicking at the casket hadn't worked. I tried.

I tried screaming too. Maybe Dave would hear me. Again, the lack of oxygen thing occurred to me. I stopped the yelling, the kicking, and the screaming. I put my brain to use. I wasn't locked inside it like I'd been at After Dark Con. I had full use of my magic. I was in a graveyard. It was the winter solstice. So, if I found the right spell, my magical power would essentially be turned to eleven.

"Move the earth above my head.
Release me from this forever bed.
Spread the dirt far and wide.
Return me to freedom on the outside."

Sometimes with a spell, there's no indication that it's working—not until you're face to face with the doctor you tried to summon.

Other times, it just works.

This was one of those times.

The casket began to shake, as if an earthquake had started around me. I almost expected to be shot out like a cannonball. Instead, my insides whooshed like I was in an elevator plummeting toward the ground. It made sense, as that was exactly what was happening, minus the elevator. I was going down, down, down, sinking deeper and deeper into the earth.

The casket plunged, breaking through dirt and rock. It dropped several feet, jolted to a stop, and burst open, tumbling me and my skeletal friend onto a cold and hard cavern floor.

I gasped a lungful of thick wet air. The muggy air was a reprieve from the lack of same in the casket. The casket was now scattered pieces on the craggy floor along with the bones.

My eyes, having adjusted to the pitch-black darkness inside that box of doom, could now make out the floor and the walls in the dark tunnel where I found myself. Next to me, my hand brushed a large bone.

Faint moonlight trickled in from above, through the hole the casket made to the graveyard above. While the casket had twisted through the ground, the loose soil above it filled in the gap. The hole was no bigger than my wrist.

Moonlight... how long had I been down there?

But that wasn't the only source of light. There were two more pinpoints, one on each side of me. Either could be my way out. I chose at random and almost immediately knew that I was going the wrong way.

The air got cooler and dense. The light grew brighter, much brighter. That wasn't right. The sun wasn't out. My insides squirmed a warning.

I realized something else was drawing me toward that light. Curiosity.

Isn't that what killed the cat?

I didn't want to think about cats right now.

I stumbled forward until the combination of light and my eyes adjusting painted a clear picture of the cavern ahead. There were some spots where rotting wood kept the walls from crumbling and others where small cave-ins had already happened. Large mounds of dirt and rock littered the floor.

I weaved around them. The light at the end of the tunnel beckoned, growing closer with every step.

I reached a spot where I knew I'd seen enough. I knew without a shadow of a doubt what was at the end of this particular tunnel.

Magic. Pure magic. This was the mine. I could feel the magic moving around me, drawing me closer.

The light became less a light and more a rainbow of colors. I found an orange rock, like something painted with glow paint—like a shirt under blacklight at a rave. The walls became speckled with pigments of orange and green, turning blue then white near the tunnel's end.

It opened into a large cavern, where the walls were radiating the light. Except at the very center—there was a hole and nothing but pitch blackness.

I stepped to its edge, peering down. It dropped like a well, hundreds of feet into the earth with only faint shimmers of light here or there along the rocky walls down to oblivion.

Where the presence of magic should have built to a crescendo, it went flat. Silent. They'd been successful in stripping the mine of the magic... until that explosion.

There was no telling how much had been taken, where it'd been taken, or why. It was gone now. This sparkling room was what remained.

I eased away from the abyss, feeling like a ball of nerves

—feeling like there might be someone standing behind, ready to push me.

Someone was.

Summer Shields and the smirk I knew all too well.

28

IN CAVERNS DEEP

Summer was standing at the mouth of the cavern, about twenty feet away from me. Her evil smirk became a sneer and then, oddly, a full-blown smile. She peered around at the shimmering walls, taking them in like a deep breath.

"Summer..." My voice was a whisper that barely carried across the space. I should've known. I should've put it together. It was so easy to see now.

If Jami Castel was sensitive to magic and Summer was too, it made sense they were in it together, using the same people and after the same things.

No, that's not right.

I wanted to be wrong. But Summer was standing right there. She regarded me, her smile faltering slightly.

"Summer, you don't have to do this."

I wasn't sure how it worked, not really—how she'd take the magic from this place.

I didn't have to wait long for her to show me. She ran her hand along the rocks, painted with magic in blues and greens and orange. The brightest of them, so close to white, were blinding.

The colors wiped away under her hand and she smiled again.

Unlike those miners, doing someone else's bidding and carefully removing the rock, all she had to do was touch them. The magic went inside her, lived inside her, and she could use it for whatever nefarious purpose she wanted.

Gran's spell had been broken since the second she made me the guardian of this place. Summer could take all she wanted... unless I stopped her.

"Summer, stop!"

"Summer?" Her eyes narrowed. She crossed the threshold into the cavern. "I'm not Summer. Come now, Constance. I thought you were a better detective than that."

No matter what nonsense spouted from her mouth, I just needed to keep her talking. I needed to think, to find my way out of this predicament.

The more magic she gathered, the more unlikely that would be—and the more likely she was to use it against me.

I looked back. I was a few feet away from the abyss. I imagined the fall down would end differently than the fall of the casket from the graveyard to the mine shaft.

"I never claimed to be a detective," I said.

"No. You just play pretend. You and that familiar of yours snooping in *my* house..."

"Wait... Agatha?"

She reached out, touching another rock; the orange glow disappeared. Briefly, her features brightened. Her face took on the same radiance.

"Not Agatha. Not exactly."

She reached out again. I had to do something.

"Stop her, now.
Stop her, she's foul."

Summer's body froze, mid-stroke. Her hand was close to the wall but not touching it. She shook with tremors, fighting my magic. And, I realized too late, she had her words. She murmured something.

A jolt of pure pain shot through my body. The agony caused my knees to buckle. I fell to the ground, writhing. It would've been easy to lose focus, to drop my concentration and let her go. But somehow, I held on.

"Unbind me and I'll stop," she said.

"No."

This was a real magical duel. No wands. No death spells. Just magic against magic. It took every ounce of mine to prevent her from reaching out and gathering more.

"Tell me who you are." I strained. The throbbing in my temples multiplied tenfold. I clasped the top of my head and fought through the pain. But I lost focus and Summer's hand wrenched free. She found a small flow of glowing rocks and pressed her fingers on it.

A new pain erupted down my spine, like biting into something hard with a tooth in desperate need of a root canal. Only the root was my spine. It shot through my spine to the tips of my fingers and toes. I seized and the rest of me fell to the ground. Desperately, I tried to keep my head high and my eyes focused on her.

"I thought for sure you were on to me. That you must know who I am. What I am."

"What are you?"

"Don't I sound *familiar*?" The husky voice shook the walls around us. It didn't come from Summer's lips, but I knew it came from inside her.

"You... were you the cat?"

"Not since you've known me. Not for a long time." It was Summer's voice again. And while she talked, the pain eased, allowing me to regain some control. "Eightball is what she named me, this iteration. She never found it peculiar when one cat ran away, an identical cat would take its place."

"But Agatha never had a familiar." I reached out with my magic again, hoping the same spell would bind her.

"Agatha *thought* she never had a familiar. I was her mother's. But to her, I was a cat. A plaything. Her mother never realized I was slipping in and out of Agatha's mind, ever since she was a little girl."

"You—you collected the rocks." I remembered the cat in Agatha's arms in that photo with Hope.

"I did."

"But how?"

"The mind is a funny thing. We shared it for so long. She actually believed I was the voice in her head. Sometimes, I even let her have the wheel. She thought she was in control."

"Why kill her?" I asked. "Why kill Jami? And Steven?"

"Oh, you," Summer's face twisted, "so naive. Don't you know anything? A familiar can't kill a witch. That would break the bargain we made. I didn't kill Agatha.

"I merely grew tired of sharing her mind. I found a more permanent solution, a suitable vessel for her—my old body.

"She was dying anyway. In the end, it was a mercy. She yearned for her death. I told her we could make it quick and easy. I allowed her the use of her old body once again. And she came down here one last time, finally taking the stones for herself."

"But she didn't die down here?"

"Oh, she did. And it wasn't yesterday either. But when I

let her go, the cat escaped. That's when I realized it knew more than it let on."

"The cat escaped..."

Summer—Eightball—smiled wickedly. "She was with you for a while. In fact, your spell hid her from me. Again, I thought you knew. I thought you were clever. But now, now I see otherwise."

"And Jami, what did she do wrong?" I tried to think, to push past the pain and find a solution.

"That wasn't me. That was someone else."

"That's just what you want me to believe."

"It's the truth," Summer spat. "As I said, I cannot kill anyone. I've never played a hand in anyone's death. At least, not until now."

"So, you can kill me, huh? How does that work for you?"

"I'll be protecting the mine—as you should've done. If you're here when it collapses, that's not my fault, now, is it?"

"It sounds to me like a breach of your deal."

"I'm willing to risk it."

∼

A BLACK SHAPE appeared in the corner of my eye. It blurred past me then came to a stop between us. It met Summer with a hiss, its back arched, its hair standing on end.

The cat—the cat who'd led me into this trap.

"There's our girl now. The new girl. Look at her. I think she wants this back." Summer's fingers ran down her body.

"Summer," I said, realizing my mistake.

The cat hadn't lured me to this trap. She was trying to help me—help me help her. The cat meowed a plea in my direction.

"I'm trying," I said.

"Shut her mouth.
This is going south."

Summer's lips couldn't move. But the throaty voice of the familiar rang out with another spell.

Magic, the bullet, the familiar's words the gun.

This time, it felt like my head might truly explode, finally forcing me to lose all concentration—to lose sight of anything but the pain.

I grabbed my own head again in a useless effort to stop the flow. But there was no open wound there, just flesh and bone between my hands and the source.

Bone.

I thought it again. The word meant something, but I couldn't figure out what.

It was something Hope Evans had said. Spirits need a vessel.

"It's over, Constance. I've won." Summer's voice again. "There's enough magic here for both of us. For us to use forever."

The lie betrayed the magic, allowing my pain to subside just enough. Enough for me to put together a spell.

She swiped both hands along the walls, taking the magic in, glowing brighter and brighter. She murmured another spell and the walls started to shake. Dirt and pebbles loosened, falling like rain.

I tasted the failure. It tasted like dirt, like sand in my mouth. I sputtered the spell from my lips.

"Your shift is over, this is the end.
Go, now. It's your time to transcend.
Rest now, spirit.
So no one need fear it.

> Into a tomb of bone,
> in your new home, alone."

Without even knowing if it worked—magic does whatever it wants to—my thoughts went to Summer, trapped in the cat's body.

> "Put her right.
> Allow her to fight.
> Spirit and body, together the same.
> Put an end to this terrible game."

I looked up to see Summer's body twist then fall. A large rock, loosened from the cavern's ceiling, grazed her cheek then struck her leg, pinning her to the ground.

I wasn't doing much better. I spelled the rock off her leg, grabbed her by the waist and dragged her out of the cavern. I got her into the tunnel where it seemed somewhat safer.

But not for long. Rocks continued to fall, crashing to the ground behind us. The earth was shaking violently.

"What's going on?" Summer asked.

"Help me," I told her.

Her weight, which had been limply heavy, shifted. She managed to put some weight on her good leg and limp on the other. I was holding her tight.

> "Light the path
> out of this shaft."

It was nearly a rhyme. And it worked. The way forward cleared. We kept moving, over the uneven ground. We made it to where the casket lay in pieces just as the tunnel began to collapse.

I reached down and grabbed the bone I'd touched when the casket fell, a femur. I knew it was the right one.

"We have to go," Summer pleaded as the dirt over our head gave way. Beside us, something blurred down the tunnel. With a fresh surge of adrenaline, we hobbled behind it and out the entrance of the mine. The shaft collapsed completely behind us.

Summer eased herself down, gasping. The ground was covered with snow. I sank down next to her, dropping the bone; its yellow stark against the pure white.

We could find our way home from here, but we wouldn't have to. A voice rang out in the distance. It was Dave. Then another, Mac. Then another. And another. They closed in around us.

The cat, now just a cat, yowled and brushed against my ankles.

"First owls, now cats," I said absentmindedly.

"Owls—" Summer sighed. "I should probably tell you where you can find yours."

29

IN WITCH I LEARN MY GIFT

Summer and Jade made their studio in a space they rented above Creel Creek Brewery, makers of fine ales and sweet stouts.

Summer tried to unlock the door of the studio with a code on its keypad, but the code didn't work. "Crap."

"You forgot it?"

"No, Jade," she hissed. "I let it slip that I went to see you the other day. I think she could tell we were getting along."

"Were we?" I smiled.

"You know what I mean. Can you maybe help?"

"You try." Another touch had revealed something more than Summer being sensitive to magic. Eightball's efforts in the mine had left the magic inside her. She was now as powerful as any of us witches, although I wasn't sure I wanted to tell her that, not yet.

"How?"

"Think of a rhyme, intend to unlock the door, and say it."

"Okay…"

"Unlock with a shock."

She pointed at the doorknob and a jet of blue spark leaped out of her finger. "Ouch!"

"Yeah, well, that was your fault," I said. "See if it worked."

She opened the door.

The room was insulated with those absorbent foam pieces all over the walls. They had a table, shaped as either the yin or the yang, with two mics atop it. A camera was pointed at it.

And in the corner of the room, in a too small bird cage, was my owl. The sight reminded me too much of Hedwig in Harry Potter. She fluttered and trilled.

"Let's get you out of here."

"I'm really sorry," Summer said. "It was Jade's idea."

"I know."

"I can't even fathom how she trapped it."

"She's resourceful."

"Oh, she's more than resourceful." Jade's voice pierced the air of the room. "Summer, I can't believe you'd—"

"What? You can't believe I'd what?"

"You'd align yourself with this liar."

"You don't know what you're talking about," Summer said.

"Then tell me." Jade blocked the exit. "Explain. Unless this means Constance is going to be a guest on our show..."

"Not exactly." Summer unplugged a microphone from the table, wrapped up its cord, and held it. "Funny thing about the show. I'm going to be taking a break from it."

"I'm so surprised," Jade scoffed. "Speaking of breaks, our friend Trish is going to be taking a break too." Jade shrugged a fake apology.

I didn't speak. I picked up the cage and headed for the door.

"Let us out." Summer followed my lead. She held her microphone in her hand.

"Or what?" Jade asked. "You going to club me with that?"

"No." She murmured something and Jade spasmed like she'd been shocked by the world's worst static electricity. She stumbled away from the door, leaving enough room for us to pass her.

We took the stairs down and left through the brewery. They were hosting an office holiday party and having fun with a white elephant or dirty Santa exchange. No one noticed the caged owl I was holding.

I set her down on the backseat. "You know... we can do a lot more than shock people."

"I figured," Summer said. "But shocking people is pretty fun."

∽

Our next stop was guaranteed not to be as fun, but there were a few things left to work out. Unfortunately, Eightball hadn't revealed every secret.

Hope Evans opened the door, looking a good deal more haggard than my previous visits. This time, she was definitely in pajamas and her cool blue light glasses had been traded for cheap reading glasses.

She flicked on her porch light and opened the door, shaking her head. "This is, what, the third person you've brought over here?"

"We've actually met," Summer said.

"I'm aware. And I assume the two of you are aware it's late at night?"

"It's not even eight."

Hope scowled at the darkness. "Yeah, well, it feels late. Come in. Bring the owl, if you must."

I thought I'd done a decent job of hiding the cage behind my back. Apparently not.

"What do you need from me this time?"

"Information," I said. Hope's living room was dim, the only light coming from the lamp between her recliners. There was a cozy throw waiting for her there, and a hardcover novel rested on her coffee table.

"Nothing new then." She took her seat and wrapped the blanket around her legs.

"It's about this owl," I said. "I think it's being used as a vessel."

"Ah." She leaned forward and looked closer at the owl. "It's possible. What type of spirit do you think is inside?"

"A soul."

"Living or dead?"

"Living, I think. I hope."

She frowned at this. "Not my specialty."

"You can't—"

"I can't," she said. "Not without risking whoever's inside."

"Who is it, by the way?" Summer asked.

"My mother." This gut feeling, this sureness, I'd felt it so many times over the last two months. I felt it again now.

"I'm sorry I couldn't help," Hope said. "Unless you wanted to ask me something else?"

"Let's say you had another vessel, a vessel you don't want anyone to find—you don't want its occupant let out. What do you do with it?"

"Bury it." She shrugged.

I'd already thought of that. But burying it didn't feel like the right answer.

"Yeah… I'll think about it."

"Anything else?" Hope picked up her book, willing us to leave.

"How's your book coming along?" I asked her.

"That." Her frown deepened. "I had to ask for an extension."

The words "thanks to you" were not said—merely implied. She opened the book to her page.

It was frustrating that I hadn't gotten the information I wanted. I wanted to know—definitively—that my mother was in that owl.

Hope isn't able to help, I thought. But immediately, my own instincts—my own gut—told me that wasn't true. I shook my head, trying to shut my subconscious up.

"You okay?" Summer asked.

"Fine." I picked up the cage, and we both stood. "We'll just show ourselves out."

"Thank you," Hope said. "I can lock the door with my smartphone."

Summer smiled at this. I started to follow her toward the door when again, I didn't feel right. I stopped beside Hope's recliner.

She looked up at me, a mix of weary and wary.

"Can I ask what your conversation with Steven Robillard was like?"

"There wasn't much to it," she said. "It mirrored what you and your grandmother talked about last time—about the mine. He said a woman lured him there. She promised him wealth. All he had to do was gather a few rocks. She was going to pay him by the rock. So, he gathered as many as he could find."

"Then he wasn't sensitive to magic?"

"I don't believe so," Hope said. "Why does that matter?"

"Because only someone with magic would know when to stop. It's why Eightball used them. It's why she used you. And Summer here."

Hope's eyes went wide, seeing Summer in a new light. "Are you saying there's another killer?"

"I believe I am."

"Any clue who it is?" Summer asked.

"It's whoever has my mother's body," I said. And I knew I was right.

Relief shone on Hope's face. She had set her phone down where the book had been, trading one for the other. I slipped it into my pocket.

I knew I'd find an app there, an encrypted app that was used to call a meeting with Jami Castel.

I knew it because I knew when I was right—every time I'd been right, ever since the gifts in the graveyard—I'd known it.

Every time I was wrong, well, I'd known that too.

My gift—I finally knew what it was.

And what a gift it was.

The owl is my mother.

True.

Hope Evans killed Jami Castel.

Also true.

30

CHRISTMAS

'Twas the night before Christmas, and the twinkle lights glowed on Dave's house. Licorice wasn't stirring. She was probably dreaming of a mouse.

Dave opened the door with care. He knew Santa was soon to be there. The girls were nestled, snug in their beds. And Elsie was picturing this cat in her head.

"Remind me again why I agreed to this?" Dave groaned.

He was in flannel pajama pants with no shirt. The only light in the house came from the white sparkle of the Christmas tree and a night light on the wall.

"Shhh!" I put my finger over my lips. "You agreed because you love your daughter. And you're the best father I know."

This was a new variation of sneaking in and out of Dave's house. It was late. Really late. I put the pet carrier down beside the other gifts under the tree. For now, Licorice was content to sleep there.

Beside the tree, on the coffee table, there was a plate of cookies and a glass of milk, along with a couple of carrots.

Dave took one of Santa's cookies and peered into the carrier. "You're sure it's just a regular cat, right?"

"Pretty sure," I said. "But she *is* special. I think living with others in her head changed her brain chemistry."

"Ya think?" He laughed a little. "Could you maybe explain? I have to live with this creature."

"I'm not exactly a vet," I said. "Nor do I think any vet would believe the things she's capable of."

"Like?"

I nodded. "She can use the portals to the shadow realm. That's how she got out to the vineyard that day—"

"And how she got here," Dave said.

"Right."

There was a portal close to Dave's house where Brad had tried to use his magic from the other side to aid my escape from the hunter on Halloween.

"That also explains how Agatha—"

"Eightball," I corrected.

"—how Eightball transported the bodies there."

"Right," I said. "A familiar can do that. But that was after Hope killed Jami."

"Because Jami figured out her secret," he said. "I still don't know how you figured it out."

"Something Gran said. Hope couldn't summon the spirits from the shadow realm. She needed help. I kept wondering how Eightball knew about Steven Robillard when it was the other way around. Hope knew about Eightball. They were working together all these years. In fact, it was Hope who set up Eightball with Dr. Hart."

He nodded through a stretch and a yawn. "Now to convince a jury of our peers."

I smiled. "I'd better go."

"You're leaving? Now?"

"I figure you need some rest." When I was a kid, on Christmas, I woke up hours before it was light out. I had a feeling his girls did the same. My gift told me I was right.

"I do," he agreed. "But first, I think we need to talk."

"Haven't we been talking?"

"Constance..."

Of course I knew what he meant. And with my stupid gift, I had a good feeling I knew what he was going to say. Only, I'd been too chicken to actually think it—to confirm my doubts.

Instead, I chose to think things like *is Dave going to ask me something big? Is it something life changing?*

I'd known this day was coming since Elsie broke her arm. I could sense the words on his lips. And see it in his eyes. I'd done my best to avoid situations like this, ensuring we were never alone together.

Why now?

Can't it wait for tomorrow or the next day... or the day after that?

I knew it could wait. But it wasn't going to.

"Dave, I—I'm sorry."

"What are you sorry for?"

He drew me in, but I pushed away.

"For everything. For investigating the murder. For every time I put your daughters in danger. For breaking Elsie's arm."

"You really think your magic did that?"

I nodded. "I wanted to meet him, Doctor Hart. I wanted to interview him like I had his wife."

"Right. And you think your spell did it to get you there?" He grabbed both of my hands.

I shrugged.

"I was going to bring you in on that anyway. I wanted

your opinion of him. The broken arm—it was a coincidence at best. She's always climbing that tree. And she's fallen out of it more times than I can count. This was just one climb too many."

"But Halloween," I said.

"A mistake."

"And the corn maze—"

"Not your fault. That's how children work. They run off. You chase them. And sometimes you're in a maze."

I struggled, trying to read his face in the dim light. He looked amused. "What did you want to talk about if you're not going to break up with me?"

"Break up with you?" His voice was loud—too loud on a night like Christmas Eve. He started to laugh then his face fell. "Wait—do you *want* to break up?"

"No. Of course not."

"You really thought *I* wanted to?"

"Maybe. I tried not to think it."

"Right. Cause if you did, you'd know." He shook his head. He bent toward me and kissed my forehead. "I wanted to talk about trust."

"You did?"

He pulled my hands, leading me to the couch. He sat down and pulled. I fell onto his lap. He pushed my arms to his shoulders then put his around my waist.

"Trust is a two-way street, Constance."

"I know," I said in a rush. "I'll be better. I promise. No more lies. Not even white lies like the cat."

"I agree. No more lies. But that's not exactly what I meant. What I meant to say is you not trusting me, not telling me what you were doing, that was my fault. Partially my fault. You thought I didn't trust you. And the funny thing is, I do."

"You do?"

"Of course I do. I trust your judgment. I trust you with the girls. I even trust you to hold your own in a magical duel. I'm sorry I didn't make that clear."

"Okay..." My voice sounded so meek. "That's it?"

"No." He smiled. "That's not it at all."

I pulled away, wanting to take in his whole face, trying to see what he might say next.

"I was wondering if, maybe, you would move in with me—with us."

31

NEW YEAR, NEW WITCH

The girls had an excellent Christmas. Elsie, especially. She and Licorice—the real Licorice—were fast friends.

On New Year's Eve, we drank sparkling grape juice and nearly made it to midnight. Dave and I carried the two littles to bed.

Officially, I was moving in the next week. I didn't have much, just a few things, clothes and books mostly. No furniture.

Trish helped me pack while Dave was at work and the girls back at school. She knew the whole story—what had happened in the mine and its aftermath. She was reluctant but willing to give Summer Shields a chance to redeem herself. We invited her to the next crescent moon.

Gran waited in her recliner until we were ready to leave. She stopped me with a look.

"A moment of your time, please."

Trish headed outside.

Gran lurched out of the chair. She wiggled her finger

and a book came zooming from the stairwell. "This is yours now."

She handed me the family grimoire. "You can have it, now that you're the guardian. I've written down everything I told you. I also wrote down the spell that I used to protect it, should you ever need it, among other things."

"Gran, I—"

"Read it," she said. "And don't worry. I'm not going anywhere. At least not anytime soon."

I gave her a hug.

At Gran's request, we were hiding bits and pieces of the story from the familiars—from Brad, Stevie, and Twinkie. Neither Trish nor I were truly comfortable with the arrangement. It was second nature to trust your familiar—or at least that's how we felt. But for now, we agreed to keep those events to ourselves. We trusted Gran and her wisdom.

Trish had loaded the last of the boxes into the back of Prongs. I got in and started the engine. Trish climbed into the passenger seat and closed the door.

"She's like Dumbledore." Trish eyed Gran in the doorway. "Behind the scenes, doing magical things with no explanation."

"Until she does explain them. When she does, I kind of wish I never asked."

"You think that's the last you've seen of that mine?"

"I hope so. I've still got to figure out a few things."

"Like?"

I gestured behind us. The femur bone stuck up from a box on the seat. "What to do with that… who took my mom's body and where they are… oh, and there's the small matter of that demon to work out this summer."

"You've got a few months. And I thought Brad was helping you."

"He is. He's trying to."

"Didn't you say your mother had a familiar?"

I slammed on the brakes. "I, uh, no. I forgot about that..."

Mr. Whiskers had barely factored into my life. I hadn't thought about him, not at all—not even after making the connection between Eightball and Agatha. My insides squirmed at this revelation.

"Well, that answers that," Trish said.

"Still no clue where to find him."

"It'll come."

A lot of things went unsaid. I knew she was going to help. Our friends would too.

Speaking of unsaid, Trish never actually told me she was fired. She just started showing up at the bookstore like it was her job. And like she owned the place. Both were true.

I didn't ask how she planned to pay for food or her rent. With my own money, I made more ads. I put up a billboard in town. We had to get the coffee business working for us.

I pulled into Dave's driveway, my new home. We each carried a box to the door.

"Question," I said to her. "If Gran's my Dumbledore, does that make you Ron or Hermione?"

Trish smiled and rolled her eyes. "I never said you were Harry."

"Not Harry? Then who?"

She shrugged, smiling. "I'll say this—we do a great job of managing mischief."

32

CREEL CREEK AFTER DARK
EPISODE 79

It's getting late.
Very late.
The creeping dread of tomorrow haunts your dreams.
It's dark out. Are you afraid?
Welcome to Creel Creek After Dark.

Ivana: Welcome to *Creel Creek After Dark*. I'm your host with the most, Ivana Steak. And as of today, I'm no longer joined by my cohost Athena Hunter.

Ivana: Athena has chosen to take a leave of absence from the show. I know... I know... You're probably as sad—or angry—to hear it as I was.

Ivana: Like you, I can only speculate on the whys.

Ivana: Why did Athena choose to leave me in the lurch... why did our friendship came to an end... why she's hung her hat with that other lot...

Ivana: Well, I can tell you how it started. She stopped returning my calls and texts. She ignored me when I knocked on her door for an hour and a half. Yes, I could hear her TV. And the blinds moved. She was home. Then we had a disagreement. A heated disagreement. She stung me in so many senses of the word.

Ivana: Well, folks, I'm mostly here to tell you that Athena has taken up with the witches. We were so close to convincing the new witch into coming on the show—we were considering allowing her to advertise here.

Ivana: Well, folks, I'll tell you where NOT to go. Bewitched Books is now offering coffee drinks. Don't be fooled by it. Don't go.

Ivana: Sorry, I'm not going to hold my tongue any longer.

Ivana: Folks, it's time to speak the truth.

Ivana: I've seen magic. I've seen witches and shifters and fairy folk. They live here in Creel Creek, Virginia.

Ivana: Stay tuned to this channel as I offer investigative footage as proof.

EPILOGUE: IN WITCH WE MAKE COFFEE... AGAIN

It had been two weeks since I'd officially moved in with Dave. I'd checked in with Gran several times since then. I was getting her groceries. The Buick hadn't been out of the garage in that time.

We were finally seeing some results from the ads. I was pleased. "That's almost twenty customers already—and it's only nine-thirty."

"Who's counting?" Trish released some steam and cleaned the wand with a cloth.

"Obviously, I am."

The almost twentieth customer got in their car to leave and another slid in beside it.

"You want to take this one?" Trish asked.

I winced. "I think you've got the hang of it."

My skills—while they'd come a long way since we bought the espresso machine—weren't at making espresso. They were in delegating and surrounding myself with people who had the right skills.

Trish rocked back on her heels, watching an elderly woman slide out of the vehicle. She hobbled to the door, carrying a burlap sack that had to weigh fifty pounds or more, given the way she labored with it.

"Mrs. Hayes!" Trish met her at the door and relieved her of her burden, groaning when she took the weight.

The old librarian beamed my direction, but she puckered at Trish, who lugged the bag to the counter.

"You never stopped in to look at these books," Mrs. Hayes said.

"I must've forgot."

"Yes. You forgot. That's why I'm here."

"Right." Trish rolled her eyes so that only I would see it.

My phone buzzed in my pocket. I stepped out of the way to let Trish deal with this and retreated to the back room. The owl was free back there. I'd bought her a cage much bigger than the one Summer and Jade had stuck her in. She hardly used it.

"Hey, Mom," I said.

I checked the phone. Ivan had group texted me and Kalene.

We missed you in Portland.

I considered whether or not to respond.

Sorry about that. Sorry I never texted you back. Things got crazy over here.

I assumed this was a courtesy—him checking in yet again.

No worries. We're headed back your way soon. Maybe we can meet up then? You give any more thought to joining?

Epilogue: In Witch We Make Coffee... Again

I'd given it no thought.

The owl hooted softly. She glided across the room and did it again, closer.

If I was going to find my mother's body and restore her, I needed help. I needed all the help I could get. My fingers worked fast. I hit send, not giving myself a chance to chicken out.

I'm in... let's meet up. I could use your help.

ALSO BY CHRISTINE ZANE THOMAS

Witching Hour starring 40 year old witch Constance Campbell

Book 1: Midlife Curses

Book 2: Never Been Hexed

Book 3: Must Love Charms

Book 4: You've Got Spells

Book 5: As Grimoire as It Gets

Witching Hour: Psychics coming early 2021

The Scrying Game

The Usual Psychics

Tessa Randolph Cozy Mysteries written with Paula Lester

Grim and Bear It

The Scythe's Secrets

Reap What She Sows

Foodie File Mysteries starring Allie Treadwell

The Salty Taste of Murder

A Choice Cocktail of Death

A Juicy Morsel of Jealousy

The Bitter Bite of Betrayal

Comics and Coffee Case Files starring Kirby Jackson and Gambit

Book 1: Marvels, Mochas, and Murder

Book 2: Lattes and Lies

Book 3: Cold Brew Catastrophe

Book 4: Decaf Deceit

Box Set: Coffee Shop Capers

ABOUT CHRISTINE ZANE THOMAS

Christine Zane Thomas is the pen name of a husband and wife team. A shared love of mystery and sleuths spurred the creation of their own mysterious writer alter-ego.

While not writing, they can be found in northwest Florida with their two children, their dachshund Queenie, and schnauzer Tinker Bell. When not at home, their love of food takes them all around the South. Sometimes they sprinkle in a trip to Disney World. Food and Wine is their favorite season.

Printed in Great Britain
by Amazon